# THE LEGE

# ARTHUR KING

"You must face a bigger foe. King Arthur's enemy was Mordred. This wood is being destroyed by Mordred *Holdings*, a European-based company. This is *Albion* Wood. Albion is the ancient name for Britain. This is, in essence, an invasion of English soil. King Arthur is fabled to return in England's greatest hour of need. You, Arthur King, must defend Albion to the death!" concluded Lawrence theatrically. He wished there could have been a blast of dramatic music at that point, but sadly that doesn't happen in real life.

"Couldn't it all be one big coincidence?" asked Arthur with trepidation.

"Do you want to get off with my sister or what?" asked Lawrence sharply, then gently added, "Sire."

Look out for Arthur's next adventure:

# ARTHUR KING
## AND THE
# CURIOUS CASE OF THE TIME TRAIN

# THE LEGEND OF ARTHUR KING

## DEAN WILKINSON

With a foreword by
ANT & DEC

**SCHOLASTIC**

*For my daughter, Emily Wilkinson*

Scholastic Children's Books,
Commonwealth House, 1–19 New Oxford Street,
London, WC1A 1NU, UK
A division of Scholastic Ltd
London ~ New York ~ Toronto ~ Sydney ~ Auckland
Mexico City ~ New Delhi ~ Hong Kong

First published in the UK by Scholastic Ltd, 2003

ISBN 0 439 97835 1

Printed and bound by Nørhaven Paperback A/S, Denmark

10 9 8 7 6 5 4 3 2 1

# FOREWORD
## BY
## ANT & DEC

Dean's a very funny man, but watches far too much *Star Trek* for his own good. I remember he, myself and Dec got into a lift once at ITV and instead of pressing the button he said "Bridge". He got quite upset that neither of us got the joke and ranted at us in Klingon until we forced a giggle.

Arthur King is his best comic creation to date and I know the books will be bigger than the Harry Potter books, by at least a quarter of an inch.

What would Dean be doing if he hadn't become a successful comedy writer? He'd probably have turned to petty crime and been damned good at that, too.

## ANT

Dean who?

Oh him.

In our *SMTV* days he used to get very irate during *Chums* rehearsals saying Cat and I were doing intimate embracing scenes all wrong. He'd always throw down the script and show us how to do it himself. Never with Cat though, just with me.

*The Legend of Arthur King* is a superb book with laugh out loud comedy from start to end. He's certainly come a long way from the days he wrote our scripts in crayon on the backs of old betting slips.

What would Dean be doing if he hadn't become a successful comedy writer? He'd probably be wandering the length and breadth of Britain with a pet monkey, solving supernatural mysteries in exchange for food and accommodation.

## DEC

# PROLOGUE

*"There are now so many coincidences coinciding with each other, that it completely cancels out the very concept of coincidence itself. And that's no coincidence."*
Quotation by some clever bloke

**M**odern thinking would lead us to believe that there is no such thing as a coincidence. It says nothing happens without a reason, so therefore things happen because there are forces at work making them happen. Right?

If you take for example the amazing coincidences between the assassinations of American presidents Lincoln and Kennedy, exactly one hundred years apart, you may get a clearer idea of how amazing coincidences are. . .

- They were elected exactly one hundred years apart, Lincoln in November 1860, Kennedy in November 1960.

- Both men were shot on Fridays, with their wives sat next to them.
- Both men were succeeded by men called Johnson, who themselves were born exactly one hundred years apart: Andrew Johnson in 1808, and Kennedy's successor, Lyndon Johnson, in 1908.
- Both men are still very dead.

Is there some Celestial Jester toying with our lives for his own amusement? Smirking at our bafflement by flukes, twists of fate and happenstance? If so, he must have had a good laugh when he concocted the series of coincidences set down in the book you hold in your hands right now. Whether you're a sceptic or a believer in the bewildering realm of coincidence, the following events do spell out a truly amazing tale, nay . . . legend.

# CHAPTER
# ONE

Arthur King wondered if it was midday yet and for the twentieth time looked at his wrist to check. And for the twentieth time mused how he really should get a watch one day. It actually was very nearly lunchtime at Thornaby's Bassleton School. Arthur had managed to get out of maths ten minutes early by faking a heart attack. His teachers were so used to his feeble and increasingly implausible excuses for leaving classes early they barely even looked up from their comics now and just let him go. "Going to the toilet" had been used so many times by Arthur that he had cleverly extended his repertoire of ideas for dodging classes to "Suffering from radiation sickness", "Having women's problems" and even "An electrical fault". Arthur thought himself a pretty crafty chap for changing his excuses so often, but then the truth rarely dawned on Arthur. His mind just didn't work that way.

Everyone knew exactly what he was up to. He was trying to catch glimpses of Gwen Lott, a girl whom

Arthur considered to be the most beautiful female who ever lived.

He knew Gwen's timetable better than she did. He knew that at that moment she would be in her fifth-year French lesson, sat by the window at the front of the class. And she was. He walked past her window for the umpteenth time trying inconspicuously to catch close-up glimpses of her beautiful face. In fact, Arthur was anything but inconspicuous as that classroom looked out on to the huge Bassleton cricket field and he was the only person on it. He walked past again and this time even managed a quick glimpse down her blouse. Result! The next time he walked past he breathed in hard to try to find out what a beautiful woman smelt like when warm. No result. Drat.

Gosh, Gwen was fit. PHEW WHAT A SCORCHER a newspaper headline would have read, and it wouldn't be a report about the current blisteringly hot heat-wave, thought Arthur. Gwen was everything Arthur dreamed of. She was tall, with long blonde hair, a cute button nose, the purest blue eyes and full rosy lips. Arthur first fell in love with her on the rebound from Anthea Turner. He had adored the TV beauty from the age of 12, but now he was a man of 13 he realized he should give up his pointless infatuation with a presenter/goddess he'd never meet and go for someone nearer to home. That's when he first noticed Gwen.

He'd even managed to speak to her on a few

occasions of late, sadly always when he was alone and looking into the bathroom mirror and pretending his reflection was her. Even then, his reflection never spoke back, which was probably a symptom of his inferiority complex. When he was a child Arthur didn't have imaginary friends, he had imaginary enemies who bullied him into doing bad things like throwing eggs at buses and smashing milk bottles.

The real Gwen had never spoken back either and probably never would because she was a mature fifth year and Arthur was a lowly third year. Fifth years spoke to no one but other fifth years, it was an unwritten law. Gwen was often teased about Arthur's infatuation with her, but she was a kind, good-hearted soul and although sometimes she wanted to punch Arthur's stupid face in for showing her up, she secretly found it all cute and flattering. Apart from when the gormless idiot was trying to see down her blouse.

Arthur was tall and skinny and had a massive shock of curly, dark hair standing high above his head. He was spotty and pale and always seemed to have a look of bewilderment and pain on his face which gave him the appearance of saying, "I don't trust you and I know you don't like me." He couldn't look anyone in the eye and always remained staring shyly at the floor. Not at the moment though, because Gwen had reached over to borrow a ruler from the girl next to her and he could see down her top again. He froze on the spot and drool collected at the sides of his mouth.

"Erm, did anyone here order an idiot?" asked Fay, the school loudmouth. She was as vicious and cold-hearted as she was gorgeous. Her short, black, bobbed hair was sprayed firmly down either side of a sharply crafted thin face. Her dark, smouldering eyes were punctuated with black mascara and precision-plucked brows. Her thin lips glistened with blood-red lipstick, far too much for a girl of 15. She was as amazing to look at as she was awful to talk to. Every time she spoke, cutting one-liners tore through your soul, making girls feel inadequate and boys depressed and wanting. She sneered at Gwen.

"Divvy for Gwendolyn Lott," Fay added. The class erupted into fits of laughter. Yes, it was funny, if cruel, but largely the pupils laughed with relief that they weren't the ones targeted by Fay's venom. No such laughter from Gwen. She sighed heavily and fastened her blouse up to the neck. Outside, Arthur was swaying on the spot, dizzy with desire after seeing the strap of his beloved Gwen's ladies' sprout pouch.* He could hear the laughing, but didn't once think it was at him. He tried to focus his mind.

"Got to look casual," he told himself. Arthur stood close to the window and yawned as nonchalantly as he could, raising his elbow to lean on the pane. His

* Thornaby slang for a type of underwear less widely known as a "bra".

6

plan was doomed to failure because the window was wide open. Arthur fell right through the window, into the class, across Gwen's desk and finished in a crumpled bundle of terrified, flailing embarrassment on the classroom floor. By now the class was reaching hysteria. Even the French teacher, old Madame Thornton, couldn't help but roll in her chair, tears running down her *visage joufflu.**

Arthur stood up as quickly as he could. He nodded at Gwen and said, "Afternoon." A speedy exit would end the incident, he quickly surmised, but instead of walking out of the classroom door he climbed back out of the window, adding to the farce. Arthur fell to the ground outside and limped towards the school's sports hall where a line of puzzled-looking first years were leaving for dinner. One of them started walking beside the red-faced Arthur.

"Why were you climbing out of the window, Arthur?" asked Lawrence Lott. He was a smallish, fresh-faced first-year kid with a cheeky grin, large buck teeth and a mop of tangled, curly blond hair.

"That never happened. Go away from me," said Arthur stiffly, without looking down at the child.

"You weren't after that fifth-year girl again were you? Everyone knows you love her. You're always following her around, aren't you? Wow, I've never

* *French slang for fat face.*

7

met a real stalker before. I'm Lawrence, by the way."

Arthur stopped dead and glared at the boy. "I am not a flipping stalker. I've never even heard of Gwen, let alone seen her. And even when I have seen her I have never looked at her. You're an idiot and a fool and on that note I shall bid you good day," snapped Arthur. He walked on.

"If you want, you can come to my house for dinner. I mean, you know what'll happen if you go over the town centre, the fifth years will only dangle you over the flyover again. I live right up by The Griffin pub. There's a chippy just near it."

Arthur stopped again and thought. The kid was right. Today's incident was the latest in a long line of catastrophic attempts at getting closer to Gwen. Everyone teased him about it, even the shopkeepers in Thornaby town centre. And he'd forgotten about the flyover. He turned to Lawrence.

"But why on Earth would I want to be seen with a first-year kid, let alone at his house?" said Arthur sarcastically.

"Because I'm Gwen's brother. I'll show you her underwear drawer if you like."

Within a second Arthur had his arm round his new best friend and they walked on, happily chatting together. First they went to a chip shop, where the chips and scraps were on Arthur, then they went to Lawrence's sister's bedroom where pretty soon the bras were on Arthur too.

They say the devil will find work for idle hands. Well, idle hands were two things Barry Guthries certainly had, but no self-respecting devil would have anything to do with them. Even devils have standards. Barry, or just Guthries for short (?), was nineteen years old and had drifted in and out of dead end jobs, open prisons and git-wringing* services since leaving Bassleton School three years ago.

Academically, Guthries was thicker than a giant's greenie, barely able to spell his own name, but mentally he was streetwise and sharp. Nobody ever got the better of him and his sarcastic, snide wit was finely tuned. If he'd have applied his time to learning he may well have done well for himself. But he hadn't and now he was employed shifting mud from one spot to another, the pinnacle of his career success, and all before his twentieth birthday too.

Sad.

Still, this temporary job had a better future than the other one the Job Centre was going to make him take. Shuffling dodgy meat patties in Burgatory was degrading even for Guthries. He wasn't THAT thick. Crikey, to work in those places you had to be the type of person who pointed at aeroplanes in the sky with wonder and dread, so as you can imagine

---

* *Thornaby slang for providing unskilled and non-legitimate services such as half-hearted car-park car-washing and shoddy, dangerous building work. The "wringing" bit comes from the squeezing of every last penny out of the stupid people who fall for these ruses.*

(unless you work in one of these places), pushing mud around a condemned wood for a few months was a far better choice of vocation.

Right now, at just after twelve on a bright, baking summer Monday, Barry was sat in Albion Wood throwing blasting caps in random directions and ducking for cover behind a fallen oak tree as they detonated. Blasting caps were ideal for the land clearance job currently under way in the wood. They were small but very powerful explosives, which literally wrenched vast chunks of mud and clay out of the very earth so they could be bulldozed to fill in the river banks. The long hot summer had reached dizzying, often unbearable temperatures. It hadn't rained in two months and the ground was so hard the diggers and bulldozers were straining to shift the rock-hard terrain. Throughout Britain, Ireland and mainland Europe, the ground was dry and parched and water restrictions were strictly enforced. Hosepipe bans infuriated weekend gardeners and Sunday morning car-washers. Everywhere the air was dry, dusty and crisp. Even the nights had an unbearable desiccated heat that was inescapable.

Albion Wood had been sold to a European company called Mordred Holdings and the fifty-strong workforce of labourers, machine-and tool-operators (and men with suits who don't seem to actually do anything) had fenced off the five-kilometre radius of the woods and were eight weeks into levelling the entire area. There had been little opposition to this disgraceful destruction of ancient woodland. The company had a good case to plead. Knocking down the wood would create fifty new jobs, the construction of the hypermarket in its place would create two hundred new jobs, and the need for shopworkers when the flipping great monster was built would create countless more jobs. Plus attracting trade and commerce to Thornaby. The council was over the moon. Backhanders changed back hands, palms were greased and the whole thing would be ready in less than a year. The only real opposition came from the usual barking tree huggers, but Barry Guthries and a few of his more unsavoury workmates soon put them right with the odd slap and the odd kick which left these loony lefties looking odder than normal.

After eight weeks of extensive legalized vandalism, the once beautiful Albion Wood now looked like the aftermath of a war. Once proud and beautiful trees lay snapped and splintered, fallen and falling, criss-crossed together like a gigantic and grotesque game of Ker-Plunk. Huge mounds of uprooted earth and stone were shifted to the tops of the steep banks leading down to the beck. Not that this small section of the Tees was a beck any more. It was no more than a trickle in places. In others a stagnant, impotent puddle, rapidly vaporizing in the scorching sun that beamed down from the cloudless sky. The River Tees itself was heading the same way. It was dangerously low in places where it passed Albion Wood at its northern banks.

Guthries fumbled in his camouflage-jacket pockets for another blasting cap. Finding none, he reached into the vast tool belt strapped around his enormous hundred-centimetre waist. He was not yet twenty, but already he looked like a man of around forty. Too many afternoons and nights in pubs and working-men's clubs had made him fat. His hair had receded so he'd had The Skull Monty* applied. He had big, dark bags under his tired-looking eyes which spilled out on to a fat, bloated, unshaven face with a small mouth and permanently curled top lip.

He found his very last blasting cap and lobbed it as hard as he could at a clump of bushes. His face lit up with glee as the bushes and the very earth they stood on erupted in an ear-splitting crack. Guthries watched with wonder as a rabbit, which had been minding its own business, passing under the bracken, rocketed hundreds of metres into the air and out of the wood.

"Get in there!" said Guthries with joy. "Another!" He pulled out a small, grubby writing pad and a tiny red pen stolen from a betting shop. He put another mark against "rabit". He couldn't spell to save his life, or the rabbit's for that matter. All together there were fifteen shaky marks against "rabit", eight against "hejog", five against "foks" and one against

* Thornaby slang for a hairdressing trick used by all balding men where they shave off what's left of their hair, trying to fool people into thinking they never wanted hair in the first place.

12

"kat". He looked at his grizzly score and beamed. Then he turned the page to another which had hundreds of ticks on it. There were three words at the top. It said, in Guthries's writing, "wite berd fingies". White bird thingies, it should have read.

White bird thingies were the strange, plump, fair-feathered birds he'd been bumping off since he started his labouring job. Only Guthries, the supervisor Mr Morgan, and a few of Guthries's equally dumb friends knew about the white bird thingies. None of them had any idea what these odd-looking birds were. Even Mr Morgan, a million times more intelligent than Guthries, had never seen their like before. But he was shrewd. He knew that if anyone else found out the wood was home to a rare species of bird, work would stop right away. He and his men would be out of a job, back down the dole office. Mr Morgan's wife wouldn't like that. She enjoyed the vast amounts of money he was being paid, and the bonuses Mordred Holdings kept heaping on him because his men were bang on schedule. Plus the payments for keeping quiet about the slaughtering of the birds and a bounty for each one killed. He was quids in.

Mr Morgan didn't like what he was doing, unlike Guthries, but his selfish, money-frittering wife relied on the extra blood-money and squandered it on garish clothes, ghastly ornaments and unnecessary manicures and hairdos.

Guthries decided it must be around liquid-lunchtime and thought about setting off for The Griffin pub for a few jars and a couple of bags of crisps. The word "crackling" popped into his head for some reason, then "pork crackling". He just fancied a nice bag of deep-fried strips of pig skin.* Yummy. But what made him think of "crackling"? he mused. Then he realized his radio was crackling. He flicked a switch on the small dust-coated device hooked to his belt and an angry voice bellowed out.

"Guthries! Get your big fat backside to my office this instant. You are in so much trouble." It was his boss, Mr Morgan.

"Yeah yeah, whatever," snorted Guthries to the radio, "I'm on my way." Morgan was the boss, after all. *Got to do what the boss says*, he contemplated as he walked briskly in the direction of The Griffin public house.

* * *

Chief Inspector Mark Robertson was a good man. Odd though. He thought the world should be a much more tuneful place. If only people sang more, the crime rate would drop – he was sure of that. And TV chefs should be incarcerated too. But the singing would be a more effective deterrent.

On the hot tarmac of the final stretch of Thornaby Road, which looked on to Albion Wood, the chief had pulled up a car for speeding.

---

* *Interesting trivia note: it takes 34 pigs with dermatitis to make just one bag of pork scratchings.*

"Please, Officer, for the tenth time, I am very sorry for doing forty-one miles-an-hour on a forty miles-an-hour road. I swear it will never happen again," pleaded the young driver. His girlfriend, who was still sat in the car, nodded hopefully at the chief.

"This won't take a moment, sir, and it's for your own good," said the chief. (The driver sighed and leaned back against his car.) "Remember the words I've just told you." The chief pointed to the girl, "You come in after second line, OK." She nodded again, unhopefully this time. "A one, a two, a one-two-three," said the chief, clicking his fingers.

The driver sang, "Don't go too fast, along the road, observe the rules of the highway code."

Harmonizing, he held the word "code" in tune with the girl who came in singing, "Keep your speed down, don't go too fast, then lives and the law will surely last."

"Excellent!" smiled the chief, clapping his hands. "Slightly off-key in places, but I can't arrest you for that. Wish I could, but I can't. OK, off you go. Happy motoring, and keep singing."

The chief walked proudly back to his squad car. The driver sighed again and slammed the door shut.

"Harassing innocent drivers for going one mile-an-hour over the limit. It's a police state. They should be out catching real criminals," puffed the irate driver.

"Oh, stop complaining, Billy," said the female. "Let's get this car stripped down and flogged."

The chief – a tall fifty-something man with immaculate side-parted grey hair and a thin, lined face – smiled to himself. He took off his flat copper-topper*, which was as pristine as his spotless blue police uniform, and got back into his squad car.

Two more citizens in tune with the law. A good start to the week.

Then he jumped when something banged hard on the car roof. He got out and was amazed to see the burned and smoking remains of a dead rabbit sprawled over the lights unit. He quickly worked out from its trajectory that the unfortunate beast must have come from Albion Wood. He grimaced. "Barry Guthries and his infernal blasting caps," he said to himself.

---

* Thornaby slang for formal flat headwear with peaks worn by higher-ranking uniformed policemen or traffic police. Not those big daft jelly-mould things the plod on the beat wear.

# CHAPTER
# TWO

It was now nearing one o'clock at Bassleton School and the pupils in the dinner hall had once again found it too much punishment to consume their burned and abused dinners. They swigged down the oddly warm, vile-tasting, crumb-infested water from the pots on the tables.*

Approaching the dinner hall were the two new chums, Arthur and Lawrence. Over the last hour they'd found they had so much in common. They both loved reading (mainly *Star Trek* books), computers (mainly for playing *Star Trek* games) and the Internet (mainly for visiting *Star Trek* sites). They both laughed at a joke Lawrence made about some *Star Trek* alien downloading rude pictures off the Net. No one within earshot understood the gag, especially not the punchline, which was "Seedy Romulan".

Yeah, Arthur had decided Lawrence was OK, he

---

* That's because the dinner ladies scoop it out of the toilets before dinnertime, and they spit in it. It's true! A bloke I know told me – his gran was a dinner lady and she hated kids.

was a good lad. Even though he was a first year.

People they passed sniffed the air and looked puzzled because Arthur absolutely reeked of perfume. He had found a bottle of it on Gwen's dressing table and sprayed the full lot on himself so he would never forget her pong.

The two new friends stopped their laughing as they entered the dining hall and saw Gwen sat eating with her friends. She curiously eyed the water she had just poured from a jug before drinking it. Behind her a dinner lady walked past and sneered.

"Sucker," whispered the old hag to herself.

Arthur and Lawrence stepped up to Gwen. Her three friends immediately giggled to one another. "Gwen, this is Arthur King. He's my new best friend."

"Oh yes, we've met. Hi, Arthur," said Gwen trying to ignore her chortling friends. "You OK after your accident this morning?"

Arthur was gawping at her like an arsonist watching a fire. He was enthralled and delighted, too much so to answer rationally.

"Bra," he said dumbly. Gwen uneasily felt the buttons on her blouse that were thankfully all still fastened. Her friends, and everyone on the surrounding tables, smirked at one another. Becoming increasingly stressed by the situation, Gwen tried to change the subject.

"You smell nice, Arthur," smiled Gwen.

"He shouldn't do. Not after the enormous poo

he's just done in our upstairs toilet, Gwen," replied Lawrence innocently. What seemed like a million stifled snorts permeated the air – then utter silence. Arthur looked at Lawrence in horror, trying to hush him with his mind because words (even the word *bra*) had now completely failed him.

Gwen was also mortified and groped for a response. "You enjoy it?" she said – instantly screaming inside her mind, wondering where the hell that question came from.

Lawrence nodded calmly. "He did by the sound of it," said he.

It was Arthur's legs that were failing him now. He swayed on the spot and made silly, rasping, choking noises. Fay was gleefully watching the pitiful scene and left her place in the slops queue holding her practically full plate of toyed-with (unspecific breed of) fish and (don't ask how old) chips. She placed it on a chair behind Arthur.

"Easy, Prince Charming. Take a seat."

Fay guided Arthur down to sit on the plate. Greasy lumps of grey fish squelched out under his weight. He covered his eyes as the whole hall erupted into bellowing laughter. He lost track of time as he mentally blocked out their scorn, gibbering the word "bra" over and over to himself. He took a deep breath and stood up, food dripping from his trouser seat.

"I am not the fool you think I am!" he proclaimed loudly.

"They've gone, Arthur," sighed Lawrence. "They left quarter of an hour ago."

Arthur opened his eyes. The hall was deserted apart from Lawrence, who was sat playing on his Gameboy, and three dinner ladies in the kitchen area huddled round a huge saucepan, cackling to themselves. Arthur sighed and walked out of the hall, out of the school and headed for home, unable to cope with any more embarrassment that day. Lawrence followed.

* * *

"Well don't look at me, I'm not squeaking," snapped Fay at her classmates.

"It's coming from your direction, Fay," said Gwen.

"Button it, Lott," scowled Fay. "But I admit, I can hear something."

"It's coming from your handbag, I think," said the girl sat next to Fay.

Fay sighed angrily and picked up the expensive Chanel bag. "Someone's obviously put a novelty squeaky ring-tone on my mobile for a laugh, that's all."

Fay reached into her handbag, feeling around for her phone. She pulled out her hand and gasped at it. All of her classmates, even the boys and their teacher, Mr Simmonds, screamed and ran out of the art room leaving Fay staring at her hand in horror and the live, squeaking two-headed rat held within her frozen fingers.

* * *

"You put Deformed Terry in Fay's handbag?" asked Arthur as the two walked down Trenchard Avenue.

"Yeah, I thought she needed bringing down a peg or two. I knew Ste Jukes still had the school rat in our classroom as it was his turn to look after him last weekend. Hope poor Terry doesn't get too much of a shock when he sees her."

Arthur laughed hysterically, a laugh he'd never done before. "Deformed Terry, hey. Brilliant. Thanks, Lawrence."

"It's OK," said Lawrence shrugging his shoulders. "That'll learn her to mess with my mates." He walked on and Arthur stopped for a second, genuinely touched by the gesture.

"Hey, I hope he doesn't bite her – his teeth might fall out," said Arthur.

"It's OK, he's still got his other mouth," added Lawrence. Arthur nodded in agreement and walked on to catch his friend up. They chatted happily as they turned right into Arthur's street.

"This where you live, then?" asked Lawrence, looking up at the orange brick street house in Sherwood Road.

"Yeah," said Arthur. "But Mum and Dad will still be at work. We can go and see Mel next door if you like. He's got a metal detector."

"Handy," replied Lawrence, without really meaning it.

*Mordred Holdings, Modern Shopping Centres For A Mordred World*, read the billboard. It was attached to one of the six prefab huts that made up the small complex of offices and storage sheds at the entrance to Albion Wood. Diggers and bulldozers trundled along a newly beaten road and in through the rickety, mesh main gates, stirring up dust and noise. Lorries laden with cut-down trees passed the other way, out of the site. Deafeningly they rumbled past the site manager's hut. Mr Morgan was the big cheese, but even he had to contend with the racket of the machinery and was shouting down the mobile phone he was holding. He wore a well-pressed grey suit and tie which weren't exactly unfashionable, but were definitely not fashionable. Pity the same couldn't be said about his awful combination of white sport socks and black slip-on shoes. But you just can't explain this to some men.

Morgan was leaning back on his chair with his feet up on his desk, half-concentrating on his phone call and half thinking about how smart his shoes and socks looked. He was around forty years old with a big bushy moustache and eyebrows to match. His nose and lips were thin and he looked like a very serious man indeed. Under his yellow hard-hat was a thick mane of greased-back, jet-black hair. All in all he looked quite the serious chap, but when he spoke the illusion was shattered. He wasn't serious at all. His thick Teesside accent was warm and friendly, but the tone of the conversation he was currently engaged in was not. It was becoming quite the opposite and all thoughts about how nice his footwear was left his head.

"I am not paying you one more penny, Mr Evans. You've been paid one thousand pounds," he said firmly. He paused while the other person spoke. "I know I'm in this a lot deeper than you, Mr Evans, but we have come this far and there is no turning back now. The damage is done." He paused again. "Well, think about that. If you did go to the media, how would you fare in all of this? You are a Council-contracted wildlife expert. It was your job to declare the area clear for bulldozing. But you found it wasn't. You found it was home to a rare breed of bird but accepted a bribe from the owner of Mordred Holdings to keep your ornithological gob shut about it. They'd hang you out to dry, you divvy."

As Morgan spoke he spotted something out of his office window. He opened a filing cabinet and took out a smallish, loaded, sportsman's crossbow. He held the mobile between his ear and his hunched shoulder and aimed the weapon with one eye closed. Not a hundred feet before the site complex, sitting in a tree, was one of the "white bird thingies". It was in fact a rainbird, but Morgan didn't know its species. No one did. The large, plump bird preened itself, oblivious to the crossbow bolt aimed at its over-sized, white feathered head.

"I'm not a callous man, Mr Evans," said Morgan as he fired the crossbow at the innocent bird. It missed its target and embedded itself in the tree trunk. The clumsy bird fell out of the tree with the shock, but regained its composure before hitting the ground and flew off at speed. "Damn it," cursed Morgan. "If I go down for this, I'll make sure you do too, big style. I have computer files containing transcripts of all our meetings, witnessed by Barry Guthries. I will not hesitate to present this evidence to the law should the need arise." He paused then smiled. "I knew you'd see it my way." Mr Morgan uttered a few more words before finishing his call, but you really don't need to know what he said as they were incredibly rude and medically impossible.

Mr Morgan saw Guthries walking lazily into the site gates. "Guthries, get in here now!" he bellowed out the window. Guthries waved cheekily and entered the hut. Mr Morgan was now stood with his hands on his hips, which should have said, "Oooh, I'm miffed," but the sentiment was lost on the cocky fat nineteen year old. Guthries wasn't scared of anyone, especially not after a drink.

"Late, Guthries," said Mr Morgan angrily.

"Yeah? That makes two of us then. You ordered me back over an hour ago, remember," replied Guthries smarmily as he sat in Mr Morgan's chair, put up his feet and took out his cigarettes.

Mr Morgan took a deep breath, trying to stay as calm as possible and said, "Where have you been?" In response, Guthries burped loudly and breathed in his direction. Mr Morgan could smell the lager. "The Griffin pub. Do you know how dangerous it is to return to a place of work, especially one with heavy machinery, after consuming alcohol? This is the last time I'm telling you!"

"Thank God for that, I'm sick of hearing it."

"I'm serious, Guthries. You can't come to work drunk."

"Oh you can, it's easy. What you do is, you go to the pub, right, and—"

"Guthries!" Mr Morgan interrupted, his patience all but gone. "Less of your lip. I wanted you back here because you were once again setting off blasting caps at unauthorized times of the day. You know blasting must be supervised by the most senior member of staff, me, at the police-regulated times of 1 p.m. to 3 p.m. weekdays only. You idiot! It's bad enough we have to slaughter wildlife on a mass scale to keep this thing going, but you are jeopardizing our very livelihood. My livelihood. My marriage. If I lose my job, I lose my wife. You mustn't put us at any more risk! Understand?"

Guthries looked Mr Morgan up and down and shook his head.

"You can't make an omelette without beating the hell out the eggs, Morgy," he said, offering a sarcastic smile.

"*Mister* Morgy – I mean Mor*gan*. I should fire you on the spot, you and your dopey fat friends."

Guthries suddenly looked very angry and altogether sinister. Mr Morgan took a step back, knowing Guthries could be pushed to violence when his sarcasm ran out.

"But you can't because we know all about them white bird thingies. In fact, it's you who keeps telling us to kill the flaming things. You're in it as deep as we are. You need us," he sneered.

"I want you and the other three half-wits to drop all other jobs until the last few remaining birds have been culled. That bent ornithologist, Evans, is angling for more of the keep-shtum money, which is dwindling fast because you keep letting this whole sordid business slip to your daft labourer mates."

"Oh, that reminds me. It's not just Pondlife, Dogga and Snooty Bruiser who know now. Silent Stu and Mr Bus may slightly know too. I accidentally let it slip in the pub, so they'll need to be cut in too."

"What!? I said don't tell anyone else!" Mr Morgan slammed his fist down on the desk. "Especially not Silent Stu, who'll probably write all about it on every flipping wall in Thornaby! And how come Mr Bus can make it to the pub in time yet he's always half an hour late for work!?"

Guthries shrugged his shoulders. "I couldn't help it. I'm a right blabbermouth after a few pints of silly soup. Soz and all that."

"Guthries, I know what you're up to, cutting your old school mates into the deal. Well I'm not increasing the culling bonuses. The more people who know, the smaller your cuts are. It was only you and I to begin with, now there's a flaming tribe of you low-life scumbags."

"You'll have to increase the culling bonuses, as it happens, cos Klepto-Cass, Planet Of The Apes, Child's-Feet and The Stain know too." Guthries smiled cockily, "Many hands make light killing, Morgy. And Pondlife knows where he can get us some real guns, not those poxy crossbow things."

"No! No more noise. Crossbows are silent. Tell Pondlife *no guns*. The last thing we want is the police back down here."

"Can I have a word, Mr Morgan?" said Chief Inspector Robertson as he strode in, holding the still-smoking carcass of the dead rabbit.

Mr Morgan's blood ran cold at the policeman's timing and even Barry stood up, slightly taken aback.

The chief glared at Guthries and dropped the rabbit on to the desk. "This landed on the roof of my squad car. Any ideas, Guthries?"

"Casserole?" said the cocky teenager, shrugging his shoulders. "A stew perhaps?"

The chief kept his gaze icy. "You being funny, son?" he asked.

"That's nice of you to say. Seriously though, look,

the flipping thing's half-cooked anyway. Bit of pastry and you've a nice rabbit pie there. Evening all." Guthries saluted and left the office.

The chief turned to Mr Morgan who smiled nervously. "Ah, Chief Inspector Robertson, what a pleasure to see you again," lied Morgan. Inside he sighed heavily. *Oh good God. Not another singing lesson*, he thought.

# CHAPTER
# THREE

"So what's that then, when it's at home?" asked Lawrence, following Arthur as they walked to the house next door to the King household.

"A metal detector? Well, it's an electronic stick thing with a big pad on the end. You move it over the ground and it beeps when there's something metal underneath. Mel said it was the law to have one in the 1970s. I thought we could take it down Albion Woods where they're doing all that digging."

"Cool," said Lawrence. "We might find an unexploded World War Two bomb or something."

"Yeah." Arthur stopped and turned to Lawrence half in the doorway. "Be patient with Mel, he's a bit old in the head. He's harmless. In fact he's a really good laugh, but his brain wanders sometimes."

"I had a gran who went old in the head. She could never remember who anyone was. You'd tell her then she'd forget again."

"How sad for her," said Arthur caringly.

"Oh she was fine about it. She enjoyed meeting new people anyway." Lawrence looked around the hall and pulled a face. "Stinks, doesn't it." Arthur sniffed the air then nodded in agreement.

"Hi, Mel," said Arthur brightly as he walked into the living room. Mel was sat in an old armchair in front of an even older telly.

"Hello, Arthur," said Mel brightly. "Can't make head nor tail of this stupid film. It's just an old black and white one about some daft old man sat in a grubby armchair. He hasn't moved for half an hour."

Arthur sighed. "The, erm, telly isn't actually on, Mel. That's your reflection. You have to press the button I showed you. Remember the talk we had?"

"Oh right, I get you," said Mel, tapping his own head. "Same goes for that telly in the kitchen does it? No wonder I couldn't get a picture on the flipping thing."

"That's a microwave oven, Mel. Remember?" said Arthur tolerantly.

Lawrence laughed. Mel noticed him and smiled a wide toothless grin. He winked knowingly. "I'm pulling his leg. Thinks I'm daft, does Arthur. Who might you be, little girl?"

"I'm a boy," said Lawrence indignantly.

"I know, I'm pulling your leg. What's your name then, miss?"

Lawrence looked the old man up and down. He was very overweight and scruffy. His clothes looked like they hadn't been washed for . . . well . . . ever. He wore a yellow cardigan with no buttons, a grubby, stained, tight-fitting T-shirt with *The*

*Stranglers* written on it, and worn grey trousers that had once belonged to a suit, the jacket of which had long since disappeared. He had longish white hair, which was swept back behind his ears, and a full white beard and moustache. All in all he looked like a down-on-his-luck Santa. Lawrence instantly liked him. Mel had that effect on people.

"I'm Lawrence, Lawrence Lott."

"Hello, Lawrence Lawrence. I'm Melvyn Haviland. Call me Mel. You a friend of Arthur's, Lawrence Lawrence?'

"Yeah, we're best mates."

"Then we're best mates too, because Arthur's my best mate. Well, that's a good start to the afternoon, a new friend. Why aren't you at school then, lads?"

"Oh, trouble, Mel. It's a long story," said Arthur.

"Ah. Didn't have trouble when I was a boy. No. We had the war instead," said Mel as he handed the boys a rotten apple each from his sideboard fruit bowl. Lawrence looked round the room. It had flowered wallpaper that looked like it had once been garishly loud, but had faded and peeled with time. All around were pictures of Mel as a younger man. In each one he had his arm round a pretty woman. Never the same woman twice either, which is undoubtedly why he was smiling so widely in each one. He must have been a ladies' man when he was young, mused Lawrence. The pictures spelt out a chronological story of his life. In each picture, Mel was a bit older, a bit fatter, a bit less handsome than in the first black and white picture. And in each one the women remained the same youthful age. Also, as he got older, Mel smiled less, and the women were further away from him, until on the last one, Mel was alone, old and fat, looking much like he did now.

"Mel, can we borrow your metal detector? We thought we'd try our luck down Albion Wood, before it's gone," asked Arthur, biting into the apple. Lawrence cringed and looked at his, before stuffing it into his pocket.

Mel was suddenly very serious. "Albion Wood. I thought it was closed to the public now, while they stole our history from us?"

"Yeah, but we can easily get through the fence."

"They're blasting up there, Arthur. You must be careful, it might be dangerous."

"We'll be fine," said Arthur.

"Don't be too sure, Arthur. The Cat's Head is grinning at the moment. Something bad is going on. The Cat's Head knows these things," warned Mel ominously. "I'll fetch the detector." Mel left the room and began climbing his stairs, muttering to himself as he went.

"The Cat's Head?" asked Lawrence.

"Oh, Mel's got a mummified cat's head in his bedroom. It's an old-person thing I think. Gives him someone to talk to – well, argue with. Stops him going bonkers," Arthur said with a smile. Lawrence nodded.

"Hasn't flipping worked then," whispered Lawrence to himself.

# CHAPTER FOUR

"**I**'ve known Mel all my life. He's never married and has no family, so we sort of adopted him. He's always been kind to us. When my dad lost his job and we couldn't pay the rent, Mel lent him the money until he got another job. We love him dearly," explained Arthur as he and Lawrence squeezed through the gap in the hastily erected silver-mesh perimeter fence that spanned Albion Wood. The trees looked so mournful now, like they knew their days were numbered and had just given up hope. All around, boughs and bushes wilted. There were huge mounds of earth piled up with chunks of trees sticking out of them, blasted from the ground and waiting to be nudged into the beck to make the entire three-mile wood flat and even. Then the building could begin.

"I like him, he's a nutter," said Lawrence, smiling. "Seems like the rare kind of adult you can actually talk to. You know, tell secrets to and stuff."

"Too right he is. I tell him everything. He listens to me when I feel odd and strange."

"Odder and stranger than normal?" enquired Lawrence.

"Hmmm." Arthur had to think about this. "I've never told anyone – apart from Mel – but I've never fitted in with other people. I've always felt like an alien. Like I shouldn't be here because I'm not like anybody else. I think differently to everyone else." They made for a large patch of unsettled earth. Arthur switched on the metal detector.

"It's all right, Arthur, lots of kids feel like you. I do too. Well, maybe not exactly like you. You're a bit of a one-off. But that's good. Feeling like you don't belong, well it's just part of growing up. Enjoy it. Don't ever regret it. If you don't make the most of feeling different you end up being – God forbid – normal. Yak! The type of person who wouldn't get the Seedy Romulan joke," explained Lawrence. "People like us read books and like sci-fi. We believe in ghosts and UFOs and magic. We have to because the real world is so flaming awful. Get it?"

Arthur nodded and laughed out loud. Everything Lawrence had said was right. He felt good that he wasn't alone any more. And he was laughing at that brilliant Seedy Romulan joke. What a cracker.

Ten minutes later the detector gave a feeble, very 1970s beep. "I've found something," said Lawrence. "Here, hold this." He handed Arthur the detector and began scraping handfuls of mud and throwing them aside. He came across a small, metal, dome-shaped object, no wider than a two-pound coin. Lawrence scraped further and found that the dome ended atop a cylindrical shaft. "It's a handle of some sort. It's stuck fast." Lawrence gripped the handle with both hands and pulled hard. It moved slightly, but only slightly. "Nope, I can't budge it."

"Here, let me." Arthur nudged Lawrence aside and gripped the handle. He took a deep breath, bent his knees for maximum leverage, and yelled. The ground around it gave way. It was coming free. Arthur grimaced and tugged with all his might. He screamed out loud, which he thought must have sounded quite tough in front of Lawrence. Lawrence thought it sounded like a woman's scream, like when they can't open ketchup bottles, but he didn't say anything. Arthur flew backwards into the air as the handle suddenly came free, followed by the shaft of a metre-long silver sword. It was ten centimetres wide and flat and a shower of mud and clay followed in the wake of its release. At the exact moment Arthur pulled it free, there was a tremendous crash, like thunder, which came from the other side of the wood. As if in slow motion, Arthur examined the entire length of the sword before he hit the ground. He landed on his back and the breath was knocked out of him.

Lawrence gasped at the spectacle he had just witnessed. "God's hairspray!" he shrieked. "Did I really see what I just saw?"

"What? I found a sword. Yes. Look!" said Arthur,

puzzled. Lawrence dropped to one knee and bowed his head.

"My noble lord," gasped the flabbergasted youth, "You are Arthur, King of the Britons! You are the reborn spirit of Arthur Pendragon!"

"Eh?" queried Arthur.

"You've found Excalibur! You have freed the sacred sword! You are King Arthur, you dozy twonk!"

"Oh," said Arthur dumbly. "Nice one."

* * *

Chief Inspector Robertson and Mr Morgan inspected the damage done to the ground in the aftermath of the demonstration blasting-cap detonation (Arthur's well-timed crack of thunder). A two by two metre hole became visible as the smoke and dust settled.

"Now imagine if you hadn't had thrown it, Mr Morgan," said the chief. "Crikey, it doesn't bear thinking about. They'd be scraping bits of you off passing aircraft. Sheesh!"

Morgan tried to remain unflustered. "I appreciate the warning, Chief, but I do know how dangerous the blasting caps are. I have been in the demolition and construction trade a long time," he retorted.

"All the more reason why I'm not happy you allow that thug anywhere near them. That lad could find bother in a nunnery. When he was a kid I heard a report that he and his brother punched a camel on a school trip to a zoo. Apparently they didn't like the way it looked at them."

"Well, in fairness, they are surly beasts," offered Mr Morgan.

"So why employ one of them?"

"I meant camels. Look, Barry's a good worker," lied Morgan.

"OK, I know I'm an old fusspot, Mr Morgan, but I'm only doing my job."

Morgan smiled and nodded in agreement. "So, you'll be off then?"

"After the song," said the chief, clapping his hands once. Morgan sighed. Why wouldn't this loony just flipping well go?! The chief clicked his fingers, "A one, a two, a one-two-three."

Morgan knew there was no arguing with him, he had to sing. . .

*"When you're dealing with explosives, always be smart, never forget tomfoolery is a dying art.*
*When not using explosives, make it plain, keep the ruddy things under lock and chain."*

The chief clapped. "Bravo, Mr Morgan, bravo!"

"I've been practising. I wanted to get it right for you." He was of course lying again.

"Stout fellow. I'll be off then." The chief saluted and began to walk off. He stopped when one of the workmen walked up with his arms full of swords, exactly like Arthur's Excalibur. He also had two shields, a mace and a lance of similar design.

"What have we here? Treasure?" asked the chief, taking one of the swords and wielding it about.

"No such luck. They're props," said Morgan. "Don't you remember, they filmed that aftershave commercial in Albion Wood in the 70s. Battle Scar aftershave. These were the weapons the actors used. They all dressed up as Norsemen, Romans, Cavaliers and what-not and brayed the hell out of each other. Silly really."

"Battle Scar! Oh yes, I remember it! I used to use that. Don't make it any more, sadly," said the chief with reminiscent wonder in his voice. "It was a classic advert that. Remember the song? It went, '*Battle Scar! Battle Scar! More powerful than a motor car! Battle Scar! Battle Scar! It's got a bite like a jaguar!*'"

Morgan joined in and instantly regretted it. "'*The mark of a man running down his face, shows he's a womanizer, show's he's ace!*'"

"Yeah!" said the chief dreamily. "You sing that verse again over me, I'll try and remember the rest of the chorus."

"Oh I really haven't the time, Chief, really. Trees don't chop themselves down and—"

"It's an offence not to sing with a policeman," the chief interrupted sternly. "I could arrest you." It was his turn to lie.

Morgan sang passionately. "'*The mark of a man, running down his face, shows he's a womanizer, show's he's ace!*'"

" '*Battle Scar! Battle Scar! Smell like a rock- or a movie-star! Battle Scar! Battle Scar! Only poofs don't use it, is that what you are?'*"* sang the chief, clicking his fingers and tapping his foot. All around the workers downed tools and smirked. "Again," said the chief.

Morgan sang again. And again. Again. And then again.

* * *

"Can you hear singing?" asked Arthur. He sat on the riverbank alongside Lawrence and flicked the trickling beck with his bare toes. It stung a bit, because of the high chemical content. He dipped Excalibur into the water and fished out a crisp packet. "Could just eat a bag of crisps."

"Arthur!" demanded Lawrence passionately. "You are King Arthur! Arthur King, get it? You pulled the sword from the stone! It's obvious!" Lawrence leapt to his feet. "God's Reeboks! Who do you love?"

"Your sister, you know that." Arthur shrugged his shoulders.

"Gwendolyn Lott, Gwen Vera Lott! Gwen-Vera sounds awfully like Guinevere, if you say it fast enough."

"Gwen-Vera-Gwen-Vera-Gwen-Vera," repeated Arthur quickly to himself. "Yup, works for me."

"Guinevere was Arthur's queen! You were destined to be with her!"

* Come on, it was the 1970s for goodness' sake.

Arthur began to take a serious interest. "Keep talking, I'm listening."

"I'm Lawrence! Lawrence Archibald Lott. Lawrence A Lott. Well, that sounds like Lancelot, if you're a bit hard of hearing!" reasoned Lawrence. "Sir Lancelot was Arthur's best mate. I'm your best mate. Only mate, in fact."

"Didn't Lancelot get off with Guinevere though? The sly creep," asked Arthur.

"Well that wouldn't happen again, because this time round she's my sister. It doesn't have to fit perfectly! This is a new chapter in the legend! Arthur is the once and future king who will return to England in its hour of need!"

"But who am I going to fight?! I'm rubbish at fighting. Last month the McCartney twins beat the living daylights out of me for nothing."

"The McCartney twins are only seven," gasped Lawrence.

"I bruise easily, so I did the sensible thing. I rolled into a ball and cried until they left in disgust."

"Michael McCartney is in a wheelchair!"

"They had that flipping Yorkshire Terrier with them. It bit me on the trousers. They shouldn't give dogs Chum. It only encourages healthy teeth and gums."

Lawrence thought for a minute then suddenly looked shocked and amazed. "You aren't here to fight the McCartney twins, Arthur."

"Phew."

"You must face a bigger foe. King Arthur's enemy was Mordred. This wood is being destroyed by Mordred *Holdings*, a European-based company. This is *Albion* Wood. Albion is the ancient name for Britain. This is, in essence, an invasion of English soil. King Arthur is fabled to return in England's greatest hour of need. You, Arthur King, must defend Albion to the death!" concluded Lawrence theatrically. He wished there could have been a blast of dramatic music at that point, but sadly that doesn't happen in real life.

"Couldn't it all be one big coincidence?" asked Arthur with trepidation.

"Do you want to get off with my sister or what?" asked Lawrence sharply, then gently added, "Sire."

"I am Arthur King of the Britons!" bellowed Arthur, jumping to his feet and holding Excalibur aloft. "I will defend England to the severest of beatings!" He looked down at Lawrence who had dropped to one knee again and whispered, "I'm not at all comfortable with that *death* bit."

The two stayed in this position for nearly a minute, which would have been another cracking place for some fitting music, but again none was heard.

"Come on then," said Arthur calmly as he tucked Excalibur into his belt. "Let's go and tell your sister she has to be my bird."

They walked on in silence for a while, pondering

all that had to be taken in. Then Arthur sniggered. "*Archibald?*"

* * *

The chief was still singing the Battle Scar aftershave ditty as he unlocked his squad car at the mouth of Albion Wood. He'd instructed Mr Morgan to collect all the fake weapons in one metal skip and he'd arrange to have them collected soon. "Sheesh, imagine if some idiot got hold of one of these swords. All hell could be let loose," the chief had said.

Oh, if only he'd been at the other end of the wood with Arthur King, a boy who was now marching through Thornaby thoroughly convinced he was the reincarnation of King Arthur. If there really was a celestial higher hand orchestrating coincidences in the realm of mortal men, he must have been getting in a lot of overtime lately.

* * *

It was now four o'clock in the afternoon. School had finished for the day and Gwen was giving Ant and Dec some fresh lettuce after cleaning out their cages. Arthur and Lawrence stood over her. They were outside in Gwen and Lawrence's back garden. Arthur thought Gwen was amazing because she still looked sexy even when she was sweeping up hamster droppings. Sheer class.

"So, let me get this right. You're Sir Lancelot, he's King Arthur and I have to be his girlfriend,

Guinevere?" she asked, without looking at them.

"Gwen-Vera is the correct modern pronunciation of the name," corrected Arthur. "And yes, you're my queen. Fancy an early night, love?"

Gwen turned, laughed and patted Arthur on the head. "You've got style, Arthur, I'll give you that," she said.

Arthur felt dizzy when she touched him. It was electric. It was beautiful. He vowed never to wash his head again.

"We can prove it to you. Come down the woods with us and we'll show you exactly what happened. Please, sis," asked Lawrence.

"Oh, all right then. I wouldn't mind one last look around the wood before they destroy it," she said, wiping her hands on her school blouse.

"Not if we have anything to do with it," said Arthur heroically. Both he and Lawrence stiffened and puffed out their chests. Gwen sniggered.

"I need to get changed first." She started walking into the house.

"Will you be wearing the white one with the little flowers on?" asked Arthur before slamming his hand against his mouth and cringeing. She turned and gave them both an icy stare that seemed to freeze their blood.

# CHAPTER
# FIVE

Twenty minutes later the three of them were in the middle of Albion Wood. Lawrence and Arthur each had very red cheeks after Gwen had slapped them for mooching in her bedroom.

"What a disgusting waste," said Gwen glumly, "These woods are ancient. Look at them now, like a battlefield."

She shook her head at the burned and scarred holes and the misplaced mounds of earth. All around were snapped and twisted fallen trees.

Albion Wood had been beautiful once. It had been green and bright with big healthy trees with well-trodden mud paths criss-crossing it. Millions of happy hours had been spent there by frolicking kids over many, many years. The very wood of the trees once resounded with glee and laughter. The steep banks leading down to the beck had seen so many nature walks, so many treehouses and camps, so many rope Tarzies.* So

---

* *Thornaby slang for rope swings, named after Tarzan. Often prone to snapping so fatter kids were only allowed on when everyone else had got bored with them.*

much winter plaggy bagging.* Great fun, but sadly now a fading memory.

"A lost battle, fair lady, but the war is not yet over," said Arthur valiantly. He held Excalibur high. Lawrence dropped to one knee again to show respect for his king. "For I King Arthur have returned to save old Albion. Along with my trusty second, Sir Lawrence. . ." He coughed. "A-Lott. We shall defeat the foreign enemy and claim back our wood. And no man shall stop m—"

He stopped talking when Gwen leapt on him and covered his mouth. They fell to the hard ground. Gwen silently gestured to Lawrence to lie down too and put her finger to her lips. Arthur was dumb-struck anyway because he could feel Gwen's bosom touching his arm. His head swam.

"There's some men from the site just over the beck. If they catch us we'll get done, so shut up." Arthur looked over the beck and saw two men, one with a crossbow. It was Barry Guthries and Mr Morgan.

"Easy, lad," whispered Morgan, "Nice and easy. Get the thing in your sights and squeeze the trigger. Don't pull it, squeeze it."

"You know, this'd be a lot easier with proper guns. Pondlife's brother knows this bloke with a bazooka. We could get the job done in half the time."

"Guthries, I don't care if Pondlife can get his scaly,

---

* Thornaby slang for economy tobogganing. This involves sitting on plastic bin liners and Asda bags and hurtling down the snow-covered banks. The only braking system available is the use of trees or strategically positioned fat kids.

45

webbed hands on a spaceship. We will do this *my* way," replied Mr Morgan.

"Good grief," gasped Gwen, they're going to shoot that bird!"

"That's a bird?" asked Lawrence, looking up at the squat, pure white bird roosting in a tree. "I've never seen anything like that before. What is it? It looks almost human." It was in fact a rainbird, but they weren't to know this yet.

"We've got to do something. Can either of you throw far?" asked Gwen.

Arthur nodded and picked up a sod of earth. He drew back his arm and heaved it with all his might. Guthries had the bird in his sight; the bolt would hit it squarely in its plump breast. Gwen held her breath as the sod of earth hurtled through the air, almost in slow motion.

"Nice one, Arthur, you've saved it!" said Gwen excitedly. She would have kissed him, but the sod flew way over Guthries's head and slammed directly into the bird, blasting it back off its perch. It spiralled gracelessly to the ground and landed in a heap of loosened feathers. Gwen was horrified for a second. "I meant hit *the men*, you stupid git!" She slapped Arthur round the head.

"You should have said then, shouldn't you! How was I supposed to know what you meant!" he sulked. "I thought it was a great shot."

"What the heck was that?" asked Mr Morgan. He surveyed the surrounding banks but saw no one.

Guthries trained the crossbow up the bank but he also saw nothing. "Might be your singing detective mate. Ooh, things are getting dodgy for you, Morgy."

"Not just me, Guthries. You're in this too. We get caught and you'll be back inside quicker than a ponce in a thunderstorm." Guthries eyed him with contempt. "I want you and the other scumbags here at six o'clock tomorrow morning to polish off the rest of these birds, understand?" Morgan pushed him aside and was about to walk back to the site when Guthries spotted something at the top of the bank.

"Morgan, look!" yelled Guthries.

Mr Morgan saw the three kids pop up in unison from behind the foliage where they were hiding. Arthur, Lawrence and Gwen glanced down the bank. The kids and the adults exchanged cold eye-contact for what seemed like for ever, but was really only a few seconds. By the time Mr Morgan and Guthries had got to the top of the bank, the kids were well and truly gone. They'd run like they'd never run before and were almost home – even Arthur, despite wasting most of his nervous energy on screaming and flailing his arms about. Likewise, when the two men had reached the spot where the rainbird had fallen, it too was gone. Only stunned, the odd creature had eventually recovered and flown to safety.

"Well," said Mr Morgan in a desperate, quiet voice. "We now have a problem."

\* \* \*

The three kids sat in Mel's living-room, eating toast and drinking very weak Kia-Ora from grimy plastic beakers. (Mel was a kind host, but his hygiene standards were lower than a student's.) Gwen thought Mel was nice, if a bit bonkers, and quite with it for a reaper-sneaker.* He had all the cable channels and had switched off the six o'clock news when the kids came in and put *Sabrina the Teenage Witch* on Nickelodeon for them.

They had told him everything they had heard and seen and he'd believed every word, even Arthur's claim to being the king. Mel had then gone upstairs to get something he wanted to show them.

"We've got to tell everyone, and I mean everyone," said Gwen decidedly. Arthur gazed longingly at the vision of beauty. By crikey she was fit. Gwen paced up and down the living room, thinking hard and try-ing to make sense of the dire plot they'd stumbled upon. "I mean, we all saw the bird. I have never seen anything like that before. And, and . . . they're killing them. These birds are obviously rare, and they're killing them! Why? Surely they can build their shopping centre somewhere else?"

"Out of the area? That'd be no good for the workers down Albion Wood, would it? They'd be

---

* *Thornaby slang for an old person, meaning they keep managing to sneak past death.*

48

jobless," said Lawrence, without turning away from Sabrina. *My word she's fit*, he thought.

"That's probably it," said Gwen. "But if we're going to stop the killing and it costs jobs, then so be it. We have to go and see one of the teachers tomorrow at school. They'll know what to do. Arthur, stop staring at my bottom."

Arthur blinked and came back to reality. "But surely that'll be too late," he said. "They said they were going to start at six tomorrow. We don't start school until nine."

Gwen nodded in agreement. "You're right. Well spotted, Arthur. OK, tonight, we'll go to the rozzers. What's that copper called who came to our school to give us that anti-drugs talk?"

"Oh, the daft one who made us sing all those awful songs. Erm, Chief Inspector Robertson," said Arthur.

"Yeah. He'll listen to us."

"Oh my word," said Lawrence as he stood bolt upright. "Look. Look at the table. It's . . . round!" He pointed to Mel's stained and chipped oval wooden coffee table. "*Ish*," he added. Then he gasped and flung himself to one knee, bowing once again to his king and best mate, Arthur.

"Oh flip," sighed Gwen.

"How many more coincidences, nay omens, must ye need, wench," said Arthur scornfully. "We few, we happy few are The Knights of the Round—"

"*Ish*," chipped in Lawrence.

"—Table! 'Tis fate, I tell ye!"

" 'Tis you being a prize plonker, Arthur. Come on, the pair of you," said Gwen, marching towards the door. She stopped in her tracks when she saw what Mel was carrying into the living room. It . . . was . . . horrible.

Lawrence was taken aback too. On an old piece of wood was a tarnished metal spike. On the spike were the mummified remains of the most sinister and ghastly looking cat's head you could imagine. Its long-dead eyes were sewn shut and its mangy fur was either gone or matted into clumps. But by far the worst feature of this grizzly spectacle was the smile the cat was wearing. It's small feline mouth was stretched into a tight, toothless grin.

"If you three are going to stop whatever's bad in those woods, you'd best be quick. This thing only grins when there's real evil in town, and this is the biggest grin I've seen it do in nigh-on fifty years," sighed Mel mournfully.

*Great*, thought Gwen to herself. *A species of rare bird is being wiped out by a multinational company and what have I got to help me stop them? A mad brother who thinks he's Sir Lancelot, an old man who thinks keeping a dead cat is perfectly normal, and King Arthur who can't keep his eyes off my bottom. You've got your work cut out here, Gwen. Oh yes.*

\* \* \*

Unlike most people in authority, Chief Inspector

Mark Robertson had a refreshing open-door policy. This meant anybody, absolutely anybody, could come and chat with him in his office in Thornaby's Bobby Boutique.* The fact that hardly anybody ever did come to see him was because he put people off by getting them to sing. His pristine and tidy office was much like any other senior-ranking police officer's. Filing cabinets, big potted plant in the corner, framed certificates, crime statistics on the wall. The only difference was all the others had a framed picture of *the* Queen, while his had a framed picture of *Queen*, the rock group. The chief admired anyone who could carry a tune like old Freddie used to. He sat at his Ikea desk, pondering seriously the information on the computer screen.

"Criminal," he said to himself. "Utterly criminal." But it wasn't the latest crime reports from the Met Net. He was logged on to an Internet music site relating news that Robbie Williams was to release yet *another* album.

A young, eager-to-please male constable rapped on the chief's open door and sang a pre-rehearsed version of Queen's "Bohemian Rhapsody" especially for when the chief had civilian visitors. "*I see some people who wish to bend your ear, they have come to this place from a place that is not here. Shall I make them go?*"

---

\* *Thornaby slang for police station.*

The chief instantly sang back: "*No, you shall not make them go.*"

"*But sir, I wish to make them go!*"

"*No, you shall not make them go!*"

They both sang, "*No, no, no, no, no, nooooo!*"

They both stopped and the chief nodded his satisfaction at the efficient and tuneful young officer. "Show them in, Trevor," he said, as he logged off the Internet. Gwen, Arthur and Lawrence walked in timidly.

"Hello, sir," said Gwen, her voice quaking with the responsibility of what she had to say. "Sir, we must report to you a great and terrible wrong being carried out in Albion Wood."

"Indeed?" said the chief, smiling and gesturing to some chairs. "Come in and sit your bots on the spots. I'm listening."

Gwen smiled with relief at the friendly-looking policeman. "At last," she whispered to herself. "Somebody sensible to talk to."

"Do you doves sing?" asked the chief, clapping his hands once.

Gwen's smile faded.

* * *

Twenty minutes later the three heroes were in the reference section of Thornaby town centre's public library. It was a few minutes before seven, closing-time, and they'd been told this several times by Ms Brasscastle, the head librarian. She was a stickler for rules and regulations and ran the library with strict efficiency. She was ideally qualified for library duties insomuch as she had. . .

1) Big tinted glasses.
2) Big unsightly teeth.
3) A horrible hairstyle.
4) No friends.
5) Never married.
6) Read lots of books.

Having just one of these credentials would get you in with the library service, but having all six got you the job as head librarian for life.

Ms Brasscastle wanted the children out for two reasons actually. Firstly, it was Monday and her responsibility to lock up the library on her own. Secondly, as she was alone, this was the night she pulled down the blinds and lounged around naked in the romance section reading tales of passion and love.*

Arthur, Gwen and Lawrence were at the far end of the library in a poky, windowed room: the reference section. They were frantically leafing through the books no one usually bothers with. Every ornithological and wildlife book, magazine and pamphlet they could find on the shelves was being checked feverishly.

---

* She was a desperately lonely woman.

"Good idea of Chief Inspector Robertson's this, you know," said Gwen. If we can find a name for that bird, and some proof it's rare, we can get the building work stopped first thing."

"And save old Albion Wood, right, your Highness?" added Lawrence, smiling at Arthur.

"Perhaps I should take matters in my own hands. If I slay the workers in a righteous crusade of glory, all will be well," said Arthur, pulling Excalibur from the Asda bags in which he'd hidden it.

"No, Arthur. They'll kick your face in. And put that thing away, divvy," snapped Gwen. "It's a dangerous weapon."

"Only for thine enemies, my sweet queen," he replied.

"You're just feeling aggressive because the chief didn't like your singing."

"Not true. Not true at all," said Arthur childishly. "But I was not flat. How dare the impudent dog say that. I should have fetched Excalibur and made a widow of his wife for such an insult."

"Bother," sighed Gwen, slamming shut yet another book on wild birds. "Nothing even remotely close."

"Hey, I think I've found something, but I'm not sure if it's what we were looking for," said Lawrence. He tapped a tatty old book he'd been flicking through. It was an old, locally – and badly – published journal of local mysteries entitled *Myths and Legends of Thornaby*. The author's name had faded in the God-knows-how-many years since it was published and most of the photos and drawings had had rude parts drawn on to them. Arthur and Gwen stood over Lawrence as he turned the yellowed pages. A chapter heading read "Rainbirds: Myth or Fact?" On the opposite page was a very old-looking line drawing of plump birds with human facial features, exact matches of the white birds in Albion Wood. Well, apart from the enormous pair of ladies' wobblers* drawn on one of the birds in biro.

"Rainbirds," said Gwen. "They're called rainbirds. What a beautiful name. But why?"

The three read on in silence. . .

## RAINBIRDS: MYTH OR FACT?

*Long, long ago, nature was respected. In the time before factories belched out acidic smoke that kills trees, and waste that produces abnormalities of nature like S-shaped fish, two-headed rats and polite bus drivers, man knew how precious the symbiotic link between animals and the elements was. A natural association and mutual dependency, which humans relied on and protected. Creatures that have now been forgotten were said to rule the elements.*

*Wind-dragons which could produce gentle breezes or, if angered, colossal typhoons that could flatten whole villages.*

*Snow-bears that could whip up blizzards (now*

---

* *Thornaby slang for. . . Oh, work it out for yourselves.*

*thought to be the famed Yetis or Abominable Snowmen).*

*Frost-spiders that would spin icy webs of frost over the land. Billions upon billions of them labouring as one to create a beautiful, colossal blanket of white splendour for a few short hours in the morning before the sunshine-cockerel would summon the sun with it's magical call, (now thought to be the famed Kellogg's Corn Flakes logo).*

*And rainbirds.*

*Rainbirds were supposedly plump, pure white magical birds that could summon up rainclouds in the sky, then dart through them, bursting them, and causing it to rain. And the ancient sightings and stories about them all heralded from the north of England, chiefly Thornaby's Albion Wood. Perhaps it was around these parts the birds naturally flourished before sending out their young to bring precious rain to other countries. Indeed, the north of England has always had a large percentage of rainfall but there hasn't been a reported sighting of a rainbird in six hundred years.*

*Maybe it was a coincidence that the myth grew. Perhaps there was some species of odd-looking bird that lived in Albion Wood centuries ago which coincidentally appeared during rainstorms and disappeared during droughts. Maybe that's how the myth built up?*

*Also—*

The three kids stopped reading and paused to take in the information.

"No, that's just too much to take in. A bird that makes rain? No. It's obviously just a myth," said Gwen.

"We all saw the bird, sis," added Lawrence.

"And it hasn't rained for a while. Eight weeks now, isn't it?" said Arthur. Lawrence and Gwen nodded slowly. "And they've been working down Albion Wood for a couple of months now, or more precisely—"

"Eight weeks," said Gwen and Lawrence, finishing the sentence for him.

There was another pause.

"I need to sleep on this," said Gwen pointing to the book.

"You can't," said Arthur. "They won't let you take books out of the reference section."

"I meant the information, not the book, Arthur. Come on."

Gwen strode out and Arthur followed. Lawrence didn't see or hear them go as something else had drawn his total and utter concentration.

"It's closing-time, look," he said. "The librarian is getting ready for bed." He was looking out of the window at Ms Brasscastle who, thinking the kids had gone, was taking her clothes off next to the Barbara Cartlands.

\* \* \*

Soon they were walking home in the hot evening sun.

"Well," said Gwen. "It's certainly something to think about."

"You believe it? You really think that these birds make the rain?" asked Arthur. He pulled a thoughtful face. "That means if they are all bumped off it'll never rain again? The planet would die!"

"No Arthur, I'm just saying it got me thinking. Hell of a fluke though, it not having rained since work began in the wood, don't you think? It most likely is a big, fat, tracksuit-wearing coincidence, but one thing's for sure, those birds are rare. Tomorrow I'm going to see the head."

"What, old Glug-Glug?" Arthur made drinking motions.

"Deputy head then. Mr Bedivere, he'll help. I may keep the rain-making myth quiet for the moment. Our plight needs all the facts and credibility we can gather."

"He'll listen, once he learns I am his new king," smiled Arthur.

"No! You must *especially* keep that quiet. Any hint of stupidity and the grown-ups will just dismiss us as daft kids. That goes for you too, Lawrence. Lawrence?"

They both looked round for him and finally spotted him running to catch them up with a piece of paper in his hand.

Breathless, Lawrence said, "I lagged behind

because I was watching that librarian get naked. Wow, first I find out I'm King Arthur's second, and then I see a woman in the nuddy. What a day, eh. Ooh, plus I found this in that book. I ripped it out. Read it."

Gwen took the page and this chapter was titled. . .

### THE GRINNING CAT'S HEAD.

*In the 1660s, Britain was once again caught in an outbreak of a terrible plague, the Black Death. It ravaged the land, leaving millions dead or dying. Coming over from Europe it was slowed by a cold snap of weather and a ruddy big fire in London in 1666. But that's not how it was finally stopped. A forgotten legend tells us that.*

*Aboard a derelict and burned-out sailing ship was a cat. A scruffy, black, vicious, sneering animal, not at all like cats are supposed to be. Not like Tom or Bagpuss. This one was a stinker. Some say this cat was the earthly manifestation of a devil from the underworld called Namtar, the plague demon. It's unknown how the wretched creature was summoned to the world of men, but it strutted through Europe leaving death and disease in its wake. Everywhere it went all living things withered and died. Even the grass beneath its padded paws singed and burned. The creature boarded a ship at Calais and the crew instantly fell foul of it, never to be seen again.*

*Bound for England, the ship crashed on Plymouth*

rocks and the unearthly feline crept ashore. It travelled across the land in a northerly direction, seemingly unstoppable. People fell in their thousands.

Then, when it reached Thornaby, the beast met its match in the form of a heroic nobleman and wealthy landowner called Sir Fraggle Garstang.

Sir Fraggle had studied the cat's devilish career and knew exactly what he was dealing with. He consulted the finest doctors and apothecaries* and they prescribed him tiny doses of every disease known to man. It was Sir Fraggle's idea to contract the small measures of all diseases and build up an immunity to each one. In the few short weeks he had to prepare before the cat came to town, he lay in mortal agony, every fibre of his body wracked with pain and illness.

Influenza, beri beri, cholera and numerous other disgusting and life-threatening ailments. Then, after three days, he emerged from his sick bed ready for battle. He looked terrible. His face was a collage of boils and sores, his eyes blackened with anguish. His hair had fallen out and his pale white flesh hung off his tortured skeleton. He'd certainly looked better, and although he accepted that even if he won this battle no decent-looking woman was ever going to ask him out again, his spirit was strong. He held aloft his sword and staggered to the edge of the town.

It came. Small and deadly. Sleek and hungry.

* Archaic Thornaby slang for chemists.

A disgusting black aroma surrounded the cat and its eyes burned red with the hatred of hellfire. Sir Fraggle commanded the cat not to enter Thornaby, or face his wrath. The cat was mildly amused and waited for him to wither before it. But he did not. Then the cat spread more disease, but it had no effect on Sir Fraggle. The cat was becoming agitated with this stubborn human. Why wouldn't he just lay down and die?! It was too much for the devilish moggy and it leapt on to Sir Fraggle, its satanic claws embedding into his face. Sir Fraggle fell back and the two wrestled for what seemed a lifetime. Man and cat locked in a bitter skirmish. Sir Fraggle's plight wasn't helped by an animal rights activist who happened to pass the scene and, witnessing a grown man beating the living daylights out of an innocent cat, jumped to free the poor creature. As soon as the goody two-shoes touched the cat he instantly exploded in a shower of flu-mucus, mumpsweat and diarrhoea. This was distraction enough for Sir Fraggle and with what little energy he had left, he raised his sword and cut the demonic cat's head from it's body. The moment he did, all the disease and suffering vanished.

Sadly, it was too late for Sir Fraggle and he passed away, albeit content in the knowledge of a job well done.

The legend of the demon cat goes on as it was said the Thornaby villagers kept the cat's head on show on a spike in the ancient church of St Peter's on-the-Green.

*Surely Sir Fraggle deserved a brass plaque or statue to honour him, but they were ungrateful sods back then. They used the cat as a barometer of bad tidings, because whenever something bad was about to happen, the cat's head grinned. Its now mummified eyes were sewn tight shut, but they said its eerie, sinister smile beamed broadly just before events such as the First and Second World Wars began, or even when mass redundancies befell local industry. The bigger the catastrophe, the bigger the smile.*

*The cat's head remained on public view until 1967 when it was stolen, just before the council were about to bury it due to health regulations and questions of good taste. A council caretaker called Melvyn Haviland was questioned about the theft, but no charges were ever brought about. The grinning cat's head was never seen again.*

"You see!" said Lawrence brightly. "It shows everything we've read is true. We've all seen the Grinning Cat's Head. We've actually seen it. So if that's true then rainbirds must be true too. They make it rain!"

Arthur stuck out his bottom lip, nodding in agreement. Even the sceptical Gwen had to think about this.

"Yes, well even if that monstrosity your neighbour Mel has is this legendary mummified cat's head, it bears no relation to the culling of the rainbirds, so let the matter drop here," she said uneasily. "Come on,

Lawrence, we'd better get home. Remember, you two, no King Arthur cobblers tomorrow, either."

"Aye, my fair lady. I must away now to plan my strategy for the next phase of our battle," proclaimed Arthur, completely ignoring what Gwen said. "Plus I don't want to miss *Coronation Street*. Till tomorrow, my chums, fare thee well." Arthur ran off as bravely as he could between St Mark's Church and its prefab church hall and disappeared into the streets behind.

"Pillock," said Gwen.

"He's our king, Gwen. Have some respect," scolded Lawrence.

"Yeah, whatever." She put her arm round Lawrence and they walked home.

# CHAPTER SIX

The next day was Tuesday. Usually only marginally better than a Monday, not as good as a Wednesday (let alone a Thursday), and by no means as good as the weekend. But the hot, brilliant sunshine made every day feel like a Friday. Everything just seemed so nice and exciting. School wasn't a chore any more, it was fun and happy. Even the teachers were in good moods. (Not the maths teachers though, they're always miserable because no one loves them.)

Gwen was putting her books in her locker. All around her were shouting, barging kids, heading for their classes. Shafts of brilliant sunshine shone through the oblong windows lining the corridor and made even the roughest of children look angelic in the bright dusty air. She shut the door and jumped when she saw Arthur smiling stupidly at her from behind it. Lawrence was behind him.

"Are you sure you don't want us to come to the deputy headmaster's office with you?" asked Arthur. "I feel as though he'll only listen to us if I tell him exactly who I am now." Even before Gwen could cast Lawrence a scowl he was on one knee, head bowed. She kicked him and he fell over.

"Probably not a good idea, you two being divvies and all," she snapped.

"You have to let us come. He's our leader, he's King Arthur, King of England," moaned Lawrence as he picked himself up. "Aw, look, I'm filthy now and it's only Tuesday. Mam'll knack me."

"Look, I want a serious chat with Mr Bedivere. Serious insomuch as mythical birds that make rain, cats' heads that smile and wassocks that think they're reincarnated supermen will not be mentioned." She paused. "Lawrence, what was that man with the tie called again? Moron, was it?"

"That fat bloke called him Morgan. I think."

"Good. Now you two get to class and not a word to anyone. I'll meet you at dinnertime at Saties* and tell you what was said." She walked off. Then, without looking back, she shouted, "Stop looking at my bottom, Arthur."

Arthur quickly averted his gaze. He and Lawrence exchanged shrugging shoulders and went to their separate classes.

Fay turned from her locker and slyly watched them go. She had heard their entire conversation and had found it most illuminating. "King Arthur?"

---

* Saties is short for The Satanic Cod of Evil – the fish and chip shop near the Griffin pub. They should never have let those Goths open a chippy. What next, letting witches open a bread shop? (Baker's Coven.)

she sniggered. She took her mobile phone from her blazer pocket and pressed a speed-dial number. It rang a few times, then she spoke. "Daddy, it's Fay. You know those three kids you saw in the woods yesterday? I have some interesting news for you."

In the site office of Mordred Holdings in the mouth of Albion Wood, Mr Morgan spoke to his daughter on his own mobile phone. "Oh yes, Fay, my princess. Speak on."

\* \* \*

"And you actually saw them trying to kill one of these white bird things, with a crossbow?" asked a very shocked Mr Bedivere. The deputy headmaster scratched his bald head and paced up and down his office. He was a tall man in his mid-forties with round glasses and a long, gentle face. He was very much an old-style teacher insomuch as he never even pretended to know what music the kids were into and, get this, he actually had leather patches on his tweed jacket elbows!

"Oh yes, we managed to, erm, scare it away before they could shoot it," replied Gwen. She coughed and blushed at not telling the whole truth, that Arthur nearly killed the thing himself. "Should we tell the headmaster?"

"No!" snapped Mr Bedivere sharply. His face then softened. "He's not himself today. He's been over-working of late. He's been under a lot of pressure. He's—"

"Sloshed again?" interrupted Gwen.

Mr Bedivere sighed and opened a metal cupboard door. Inside, cocooned in a sleeping bag, was Mr Tarrant, the headmaster. He was fast asleep, clutching an empty beer tin. Mr Bedivere smiled sadly and closed the door.

Incidentally, it was Mr Tarrant, in one of his less lucid states,* who designed the school coat of arms. It was a shield depicting an old-style teacher's mortar-board hat atop a smiling donkey. He'd even penned the school motto underneath: *In Defence I Offer Truth.* The sign writer, when making the shield, couldn't fit all the maxim on, so he'd settled for an abbreviation. Mr Bedivere shuddered each time he looked at the design, a hat-wearing donkey and the abbreviation *I.D.I.O.T* underneath.

"One thing worries me about your story, Gwen. Well actually *two*, if I'm brutally honest. One. That site employs a lot of local workers. Our own Fay Morgan's father is the site manager."

Gwen's eyes widened at this revelation. Morgan! Of course. Why hadn't she made the connection.

Mr Bedivere continued. "The other thing is your fellow witnesses. Your brother Lawrence and . . . him. Arthur King. He's a good kid and all, but he's hardly credible. He's a few poos short of a full toilet, isn't he?"

Gwen bit her lip and decided to try to paste over Arthur's involvement. "If we could just raise

* *Hammered, he was.*

67

awareness to the birds living in the wood it'd be enough to get the ball rolling," she suggested.

Mr Bedivere clicked his fingers. "Hang on. I've just thought of something. The Douglas Bader School Juniors have got clearance for one last nature walk in the wood before they finish bulldozing. It's this afternoon. We could join them. And if we can get the *Gazette* and telly there too we could make an announcement then."

"Really?" asked Gwen, her heart beating fast. "You really think they'd listen to *us*?"

"Gwen, I haven't seen these creatures, and it's quite a story, but I trust you. You're a grade-A student and more importantly, you have a kind heart. I believe in you. Let's do it." Gwen's chest swelled with pride. He smiled at her sympathetically. "I wasn't always an old slaphead you know. I was young and idealistic once. I once spent a summer on a hippy commune. Don't tell anyone, but I once even smoked a salmon. I didn't inhale though."

Gwen gave an unsure, but polite laugh back and left Mr Bedivere to remember his wild youth.

Within the hour the deputy head had notified the the *Evening Gazette* and the nearest telly station, Tyne Tees. Thankfully it was a slow news day so they were glad of the story.* Everyone would meet in Albion Wood on the banks of the Tees at precisely two

---

* *They were relieved they wouldn't have to lead with the pathetic "Nut Allergy Sufferer Poorly After Eating Nuts".*

o'clock. Gwen hastily prepared and distributed leaflets telling teachers and pupils alike of the event. There was a real buzz of excitement throughout the school, like when there's a fire drill or a fight.

She found Arthur and Lawrence in the boys' toilets. They had borrowed T-squares from the technical drawing labs and were fencing with them. By now their "swords" were chipped and splintered and both boys were breathless and sweaty but still they fought on hacking madly at one another.

"Well, I suppose it's better than smoking in the toilets. I mean smoking will kill you. Trying to lop off each other's heads is a giggle by comparison," smirked Gwen as she entered the toilet.

"Wench, thou should not interrupt thine king whilst he be preparing for the forthcoming battle an' that!" bellowed Arthur.

"Oh shut up, you pillock. Listen, I have to speak with you. I need your total and utter assurance that you won't act like a complete pair of PG Tips chimps this afternoon at the press conference."

Lawrence and Arthur eyed each other slyly and smirked.

"I think, good lady, thou hast lost thine marbles. Surely my people will listen to their king and not such a mere slip of a tart," said Arthur majestically.

Gwen reached out and grabbed Arthur's left Dimmock* through his shirt and twisted it.

---

* *Gardener's slang for nipple.*

"One word and I'll do the pair of you, understand?'

"Yup, no prob," said Arthur, gasping in pain.

Gwen glared at Lawrence, who smiled nicely and held up his hand in surrender.

"Glad we understand one another." Gwen shook her head and left.

There was a pause as the boys took in what she said. Then, completely ignoring it, they battled on with their T-squares.

# CHAPTER
# SEVEN

I t was approaching two o'clock in the blisteringly hot afternoon and a large crowd of people was gathering in the wide open tract of land between the north side of Albion Wood and the banks of the River Tees.

This roughly terrained patch of land was once the gathering spot for motor-cross riders as they stopped to swap tall tales of fantastic stunts and eluding the police, who should have been out catching criminals rather than spoiling kids' fun. Sadly those days were nothing more than a fading memory.

Everyone from the Bassleton School, and the Douglas Bader Junior and Infant Schools had turned up. There were hoots of laughter, rough and tumble fun fights and cheeky swearing, but that's what happens when teachers are allowed in pubs at lunchtimes. The pupils shook their heads in shame. Hundreds of Thornaby residents were swarming in through the trees too, eager to find out what all the palaver was about.

Stood by the riverbank, facing the swelling crowd,

was Mr Bedivere. He sighed and huffed, trying not to get annoyed by the constant abuse and threats from Barry Guthries and co.

"You are so dead, Bedivere. You're trying to take away our jobs. You've got it coming, pal," sneered Guthries.

"Oh shut up, Guthries. You didn't scare me when you occasionally turned up at school and you don't now. That goes for all of you," retorted Mr Bedivere, gesturing to the motley crew of labourers stood with Guthries. The teacher, like all the others, had wasted five years trying to cope with these hooligans and had hoped never to clap eyes on them again once they left school. Worst of all the collected bad memories stood there was the slimy and repulsive Pondlife. A skinny, aquatic-looking little thug with scaly skin and greasy hair. His face was oval shaped and his eyes so far apart he claimed he could see in two different directions at once. He really did look like he'd just slithered out from beneath a slimy, moss-covered rock.

"Didn't I scare you, sir?" asked Pondlife, feeling a bit dejected.

"No, you just gave me nightmares."

Pondlife smiled and nodded in appreciation. Guthries's gang consisted (and always had done) of:

Pondlife. See description above.

Dogga. So named because he bit big dogs as a child.

A vicious, fat nineteen year old who was still quite partial to a nibble on the odd Rottweiler.

The Stain, (aka Billy The Skid). Christened because everything he wore was filthy, even brand new clothes. Theory was that if you gave him a suit made from stain-proof material and certified un-stainable by the Professor of Staining from Teesside University, The Stain would stain it. He also boasted he'd worn the same pair of pants, unwashed, since he was six, hence his other nickname Billy The Skid.

Child's-Feet. an immensely fat lad with the tiniest feet you have ever seen. His mother still bought her nineteen-year-old son's shoes at Pedifoot's Under-Fives Footwear in Stockton.

Snooty Bruiser. a very upper-class-looking youth with immaculately pressed overalls and voice to match. He was small, with a bouffant hairdo, rather like a poodle's, and by far the most cruel and loathsome individual you could meet.

Klepto-Col. A bald and devious-looking person. So-named because he would nick anything that wasn't nailed down. And most things that *were* nailed down. And the nails.

Planet Of The Apes. Purely because he looked like a chimpanzee. His nickname was reinforced by his party trick of peeling a banana with his feet.

Silent Stu. He hadn't uttered a single word for two years, since the death of his beloved tortoise Arnie. As a sign of respect he took a vow of silence and would only communicate by writing down his words on walls, bus shelters, passing strangers etc. He'd worshipped Arnie so much he now used his empty shell as a cigarette case.

Mr Bus. Always mentioned last, and by all means least. Mr Bus had never been on time for anything in his life except the pub (and only because he set off two hours earlier than anyone else). Born a month late, Mr Bus seemed like he had dedicated his life to tardy timekeeping. He hadn't, it was a natural gift. They say of him that when he dies they'll have to bury an empty coffin because he won't be on time for his own funeral.

The rest of the labourers, another twenty or so, hadn't achieved a nickname from Guthries as yet. They were new boys and had to settle for the O-treatment. This was done by shortening their surnames and sticking an "O" on the end. The likes of Mark Harrison, Andy Patterson and Marcel Di'Pablo were now Harrio, Patto and Pablo-o. They would be properly nicknamed once Guthries was convinced of their loyalty to him. They were just as unpleasant and foul-looking as the core of his gang, so it wouldn't be long.*

"Look, I'm sure this can all be easily sorted out, Mr Bedivere," said Mr Morgan, desperately trying to hide the quiver in his voice. He was nervous, very nervous. "This lovely girl, although quite overbearing, has made up this fanciful tale about rare birds with human faces for a bit of attention. Go on, admit it, pet."

Fay was stood next to her father. She sneered at Gwen.

"Yes, Lott. If you want some attention from men other than divvy third years, there are easier ways, you know. Try some make-up," said Fay sarkily. She smiled and winked at the labourers. They gave a collective sound which was a cross between bulls and broken car engines. Mr Morgan gave them a firm look, which they ignored.

"Tart," mouthed Gwen. Then she spoke aloud: "These work, you know." She pointed to her eyes and then to Guthries and Morgan. "I saw you and you trying to kill that bird with a crossbow. I saw you!"

"And that is good enough for me, Mr Morgan," said Bedivere. He checked his watch. "Where are the media?"

"There are no rare birds in this wood. Sheesh! You'd take the word of some snot-nose over mine?"

---

* Incidentally, it was the O-treatment idea that had caused a young worker called Anthony Holme to leave the job after only an hour.

added Mr Morgan, shuffling anxiously on the spot. "Kids are stupid, Bedivere. They should not be listened to, ever. Ever, ever, ever!"

"Dad," said Fay greasily.

"Yes, my angel, I'm listening," replied Morgan, turning like lightning to his beloved daughter.

"Give me some money, I want an ice cream on the way home. I don't suppose we'll be here long."

In an instant Morgan had pulled out his wallet, taken out a ten-pound note and handed it to Fay, and all with one hand. He'd had lots of practice handing over money to his wife and daughter and was now quite expert at it.

"Don't be too sure, Fay. Here come the cavalry," said Mr Bedivere as he nodded to the Tyne Tees Television presenter and the equipment-laden cameraman desperately trying to keep up with him. Behind them were a photographer and journalist from the *Evening Gazette*.

"Flipping heck," rasped Pondlife. "It's only Pontop Pike!"

And it *was* – the north-east telly veteran himself. The pupils nudged each other excitedly. They'd never seen a mega-star in the flesh before. Pondlife ran forward and offered his scaly webbed hand to the newscaster.

"This is an honour, Pikey. To think that I would ever meet a legend. A TV God! Pontop flaming Pike, man of the people!" said Pondlife. The newscaster cringed and turned away.

"Toby," he snapped at the cameraman. "If any one of these peasants tries to touch me again, stab it." Pontop stepped over to Mr Bedivere. "OK, you've got two minutes, slaphead. Let's hear it. Roll it, Toby."

The deputy head sprang to life. "Friends and good people of Thornaby," he said, "I have it on good authority that a grave injustice is being carried out in the name of progress in our happy little town. Mordred Holdings is butchering an as yet unknown species of rare bird in Albion Wood."

The crowd gasped. Barry Guthries shook his head, raised his right leg and broke wind loudly. The crowd laughed. Guthries looked smug.

"Probably the most eloquent thing Barry Guthries has ever come out with," retorted Mr Bedivere.

The crowd bellowed with laughter this time. Guthries found himself blushing. He'd never liked Bedivere.

Gwen produced a rough sketch she had made of the rainbird and held it up for everyone to see.

"Yesterday," she said, "I and –" she thought for a second, then continued – "I alone saw Mr Morgan and this Barry Guthries person trying to kill one of these rare birds with a crossbow. I believe it to be a rainbird." The crowd gasped. (Gasping and laughing was their entire range.) "It is my belief they've been slaughtering these birds since work began here eight weeks ago. They knew if the public ever found out about the birds, building work would stop and

Albion Wood would be saved and made into a bird sanctuary. But money is more important to these men. What they have done is evil and must be stopped." The crowd booed (which made a nice change). "Are you with us?" added Gwen. The crowd cheered and pointed angrily at Mr Morgan and the labourers.

"Call the rozzers!" someone shouted.

"Smash the diggers!" yelled another.

"Hang the baddies!" yelled Pondlife.

Guthries kicked him hard. "You are one of the baddies, you dipstick."

"Oh yeah, soz," he answered dumbly. Then he shouted, "It's all lies! Lies! None of it's true! We've only killed a few hundred anyway!' Mr Morgan kicked him this time. (Child's-Feet would have loved to kick someone like that, but this was a luxury only men with normal-sized feet could enjoy. He sulked quietly to himself.)

Mr Morgan was terrified by now. He looked around for gaps in the crowd to make a quick getaway. Blast! There were none. They'd tear him a new set of nostrils if he tried to escape.

"Wait!" shouted Fay. "Before we make up our minds, let's have some more proof! Are Arthur King and Lawrence Lott here?"

The two stepped forward and Gwen's heart sank. They were wearing cloaks which Gwen recognized as her mum's best bath towels. Arthur also had a crown made from two of her old toy tiaras

Sellotaped together. *They've been in my room again*, she thought.

"Aye, wench, we be here," said Arthur heroically, Excalibur in his hand. Lawrence had a brightly coloured plastic sword in a scabbard fastened round his waist. (It was the best he could do for the moment.)

"Have you anything to add to this pack of ridiculous lies, Arthur? Maybe you could tell us why you and Lawrence have towels on your backs?" said Fay, smiling slyly at Gwen. Gwen winced and prayed Arthur would keep his gob shut.

"Saves time when we want to sunbathe," said Lawrence with a smirk.

The crowd laughed again. Gwen's hopes were raised slightly and she mouthed a plea for silence to Arthur. He nodded knowingly and mouthed the words, "It's OK, trust me," to her. Gwen sighed with relief. Arthur stepped forward and raised his sword.

"Good people of Thornaby, bow down to your leader, King Arthur!"

Lawrence fell to one knee and bowed his head again. The crowd fell silent and there was a very uneasy pause. Gwen's entire world collapsed in front of her. Lawrence stood up and pulled out his plastic sword.

"Know ye not your king when you see him? I, Sir Lawrence-a-Lott, saw him raise Excalibur from the ground with mine own eyes! 'Tis King Arthur! He is back to lead us to glory. Are you with us against the evil of Mordred?"

No response.

"I'll get cross," snapped Arthur.

"Please, you two. Don't," begged Gwen.

Lawrence raised his hand to silence her.

"These rainbirds actually make it rain! We read it in a book!"

"It's true," added Arthur. "Because I know this bloke, right, and he's got a cat's head on a stick. And it's grinning at the moment."

Gwen felt like throwing up. Mr Morgan could have kissed Arthur and Lawrence. One by one the crowd chuckled, then giggled, then burst out into fits of belly laughter. This was better than Fay had hoped for. Mr Bedivere was fuming with rage. He had been tricked! Tricked by Gwen Lott. Stabbed in the back. This would be the last time he'd ever trust a child. He could see that today's mini-school-outing would go down in Bassleton School history as being as bad an idea as Mr Tarrant's idea of holding a School Beer Festival.*

Pontop Pike sighed and said, "Get some shots of the loonies and we'll call it a day. It'll do as an amusing '*and finally*' item." The news man walked away pushing an autograph hunter out of his path.

As best they could, in between gasping for breath

---

* It had left fifteen pupils in hospital with alcohol poisoning and thirty eight in police custody for being drunk and disorderly.

due to laughing, the *Gazette* reporter scribbled the story down as the photographer took shots of Arthur and Lawrence posing majestically. The crowd began to disperse. What a great afternoon's entertainment.

One of the last to go and still trembling with anger, Mr Bedivere grabbed Excalibur from Arthur's hand and threw it into the river. Arthur was too indignant with rage to form a protest.

"You two, my office, nine o'clock tomorrow morning." He glared at Gwen, "And as for you, Miss Lott, don't bother turning up at all. You're expelled." He stormed off. Gwen had no reply. She slumped down on to the ground and started to cry. Arthur noticed Gwen and his face softened. He knelt and put his arm round her.

"Gwen, come on, don't cry. And can you go and get my sword for me?" That was all he said because Gwen's fist slammed hard against the side of his face, bowling him over.

# CHAPTER
# EIGHT

"Did you see what he did to Excalibur? Did you?" asked Arthur for the tenth time.

Gwen sighed and ignored him for the tenth time.

Lawrence answered, "Aye, my lord, I did." But by now even he was losing the plot. The three of them sat alone on the banks of the River Tees and glumly watched the brilliant sunshine form colourful patterns on the polluted water. It was quite beautiful.

"I shall have his ears for ear-muffs, the scurvy dog," ranted Arthur.

Gwen snapped, "Pack it in, Arthur, you've done enough damage today. You can drop your stupid King of England act right now. You're just a very silly little boy."

Arthur muttered something under his breath.

"I *heard* that!" screamed Gwen. "You ever call me a treacherous harpy again and I'll ram my fist so far down your throat I'll punch you in the bowels! You have got me expelled from school and you still don't see what a complete wally you are! I am *expelled*!"

"You think you've got problems. How am I going to get my sword back?" moaned Arthur. Gwen's eyes bulged. She shook with anger as she tried to decide which bit of Arthur to beat up first.

"Of course, what Mr Bedivere did only goes to strengthen our claim. In legend it was the knight Bedivere who threw Excalibur into the lake," said Lawrence nonchalantly.

"Oh brother!" said Gwen, slapping her forehead.

"Yeah?" came Lawrence.

"And I suppose any minute now the lady of the lake is going to hold the sword up out of the river and return it to him is she?" raged Gwen.

Arthur seemed distracted.

"You mean like this?" he said.

Gwen and Lawrence looked to the centre of the river and did indeed see the sword held in a female hand.

"Yeah, just like that – *oh my word*!*" yelped Gwen in sheer astonishment.

"God's toothbrush! It's the lady of the lake!" exclaimed Lawrence.

The three gasped gasps aplenty as the sword rose higher and higher. The female hand became an arm clad in a tight black rubber covering, as was the head when it appeared. Then a glass face-mask followed by an entire female body, complete with oxygen

* Actually what she really said is too rude to print.

tank and flippers, began walking towards them. The three dared hardly breathe as the thing stood over them silently for a moment. It then removed its face mask to show an elderly lady's face, kind but angry. It spoke.

"Which bloody idiot threw this? It gave me a fair crack on the nodder."

\* \* \*

"I'm sorry for snapping," said Lynn, "And for spooking you like that. Must have been a right sight that, me walking out of the river with your sword."

"Indeed 'twas, good lady of the lake," said Lawrence with awe.

"Oh I aren't no lady of the lake, Lawrence, the water brings on my arthritis something wicked. No, I thought I'd have one last go at finding something. Some type of plant, bug, fish anything that might be remotely endangered or rare, so I could save old Albion Wood."

"No luck then?" asked Gwen.

"Afraid not, Gwen. I came across a 1970s Woolco shopping trolley, but that's hardly enough to stop Mordred Holdings in their tracks." She sighed and smiled sadly at the vandalized trees. "I used to spend all my time here when I was little. It's hardly changed for a thousand years."

"God's swimming trunks! How old are you, madam?" asked Lawrence. Gwen kicked him and grimaced. Lynn laughed.

"I mean it's hardly changed until now," she sighed. "Hooligans."

Lynn had taken off her scuba gear and was sat in a pair of shorts, Greenpeace T-shirt and bare feet. She was over sixty years old at least, but looked good for her age.

*Must have spent quite a lot of time underwater*, thought Arthur.

Lynn Preston had short, cropped grey hair and despite her thin and wrinkled face, her eyes were bright and young, mischievous and on fire. She had a real air of stamina about her. Lynn looked like she could beat the living daylights out of a hard lad, then knit him a nice woolly jumper by way of an apology before he regained consciousness.

She was sat with Arthur, Lawrence and Gwen on the riverbank. They had been chatting for a few hours and were getting on famously. Lynn liked these kids, especially Arthur and Lawrence. She loved weirdos, being one herself. She'd even taken their King of England claim on the chin and called him "my lord" a few times. Lynn was also very intrigued by Gwen's more down to earth revelation about the white birds, as she'd seen glimpses of such a bird, but never got close enough to observe the creatures in detail. She knew all about the magical legend of the rainbirds and she'd even written about them in a book she'd put together many years ago called *Myths and Legends of Thornaby*. She didn't mention this because no one bought the book and it went instantly out of print.

"Well, Lynn, what do you think. Could you get some of your contacts interested in the wood? You know, Friends of the Earth, erm, hunt saboteurs, people who tie themselves to trees to stop them being chopped down," asked Gwen.

"Nutters," offered Arthur. Lynn smiled and looked across the river and sighed.

"I'd like to help, really I would. But I'm afraid those nutters, as Arthur calls them, regard me as a bit of a liability. They found my measures a tad extreme. Like when I trapped a workman in a Portaloo and hung him upside down with his own crane. He was trying to fill in a pond though. OK, it might have been in his own garden, but nature should be allowed to thrive anywhere."

Arthur and Lawrence exchanged looks.

"That, on top of all the other similar incidents, has made these groups a bit wary of me. And the police. . ." Lynn's voice tailed off slightly.

"You mean, you're in trouble or something?" asked Lawrence.

"Trouble? Goodness me, no. Trouble indeed," laughed Lynn. "No, no, no. I'm wanted by the police, sure, but trouble? No. My conscience is clear. Maybe not about the shoplifting though. . ." Her voice really tailed off this time.

Gwen dropped her head in her hands. *Great*, she thought, *the first vaguely sensible person to enter the goodies' side and she's a wanted criminal.*

"I can suggest some contacts you could make, and

give you some protesting tips to slow up the demolition of the wood. If that would help," said Lynn.

"Good. Let's do that then," said Arthur, standing up. "We shall regroup at Camelot."

"Where?" asked Lynn.

"Arthur's next-door-neighbour's house," added Lawrence.

The four began walking back to Sherwood Road. Gwen lagged behind, pondering what she could tell her mum and dad about there being no need for her to set her alarm clock in the morning any more. Arthur and Lawrence chatted to Lynn, eager to hear more about her fascinating life and exploits.

"I really wish you had been the lady of the lake, Lynn. I honestly feel you belong in our happy band somewhere," remarked Arthur. Lynn put her arms round the boys.

"I'm just glad to meet a couple of young eccentrics for a change. Young people are so boring these days. It's all about looking good and mobile phones. You're good lads, and if you say you're the Knights of the Round-ish Table, then I'd pledge my allegiance to you any day."

Arthur and Lawrence smiled up at her.

As the four walked on, the boys gave Lynn a demonstration of medieval sword fencing using bits of twentieth-century council fencing. But it was cut short when Arthur accidentally hit Lawrence's knuckle and made him cry. After a cuddle from

Lynn the noble warrior was fine. She gazed around Arthur's street and sighed again. "Well, this is all new and spanking, isn't it."

"New?" asked Arthur, "These houses have been here donkey's years, my dad says. How long have you been out of Thornaby, Lynn?"

She looked thoughtful for a second.

"Oh, about the same time. Too many memories. Too much heartache. I've lost too many people that were dear to me. But hey, you don't want to hear the sad ramblings of an old woman." And she was right. Arthur, Lawrence and Gwen had walked off a good ten metres. Lynn ran to catch them up. "You see, I heard about Albion Wood being demolished when I was living in London. I was running a snail sanctuary in Chiswick. I was horrified. I had to do something. That's why I returned."

"What about the snails?" asked Arthur.

"Oh, I flogged them to a French restaurant."

Lynn stopped with the others outside Mel's house. Arthur lead them in.

"Should we wipe our feet?" enquired Lynn.

"Only when you leave," informed Lawrence.

In the living room Mel was sat holding his stomach and laughing hysterically at the news report on Tyne Tees Television. Pontop Pike was telling the tale of a hoax news conference held in Thornaby's Albion Wood where a group of mischievous youngsters had made up a silly story about magical rare birds being killed. The funniest thing was the two boys claiming to be Knights of the Round-ish Table. They showed Arthur's and Lawrence's images again, this time in slow motion with the Moody Blues' song "Nights in White Satin" playing over for added comic effect. Mel was by now in tears and they had to wait until he'd calmed down sufficiently to speak to him. Then, when Mel dried his eyes and focused on the four, his laughter stopped in an instant. Both he and Lynn gasped in unison at the sight of one another.

Arthur spoke. "Mel, this is Lynn Preston. We met her down the wood."

Mel and Lynn ran towards each other and embraced.

"My giddy aunt. Is it really you, Lynn? After all these years? Have you come back to me?" asked Mel, his eyes filling with tears, but this time tears of emotion, not laughter.

Arthur continued, "Lynn, this is Mel, Mel Haviland. It was Mel who loaned us the metal detector in the first place."

"Oh Melvyn, I never thought I'd see you again. I thought you'd be married off or living somewhere else, or more than likely dead," said Lynn, she too of watery eye.

"Mel, Lynn has a history of saving natural sites like Albion Wood. She may be able to help us," said Arthur.

"Arthur," sighed Gwen, "I think it's a pretty safe bet they've met already, don't you?"

"Huh?" replied Arthur. He noticed Mel and Lynn kissing. "Oh, right. I get you."

# CHAPTER
# NINE

O nce again the Knights of the Round-ish Table were sat about Mel's living room drinking juice from grubby beakers. The sun was fading from the sky as Gwen leant against the window, peering silently out into the garden. She slid her face from the glass and transferred twenty years of dirt from the glass to her cheek without knowing it. She wouldn't have cared. The main thing on her mind, even before the poor endangered birds, was how the flip was she going to break the news to her parents that she had been expelled from school. Even worse, she'd have to endure endless hours of daytime TV just to fill the boredom. She sighed. "Stop looking at my bottom, Arthur," she said without turning round.

Quickly, Arthur turned back to Mel and Lynn, who were explaining their shared past to him and Lawrence.

Mel said, "Lynn was researching some book or other and wanted to know all about the cat's head. Then we fell in love."

"That's me there in that first picture," said Lynn,

pointing up to the black and white photo. In it she and Mel were hugging and laughing and made a happy-looking couple. "Course, Mel's smiling because, unbeknownst to me, he'd just been with another girl behind my back."

"Hmmmm," said Mel dejectedly as he looked down ashamedly.

"Some horrible little slapper with a stupid name. Feline or something. Morals of an alley cat," sneered Lynn. "Went with every bloke but her own. After I found out I left the area. Went to live all over the shop. Communes. Squats. You name it. I joined one flower-worshipping cult and ended up changing my name to Star-Pansy. Silly cow, hey?" sighed Lynn with a smile.

"But you're back now, aren't you, Lynn? We could go out dancing tonight if you want," said Mel, looking up hopefully. "Remember the old Fiesta in Stockton?"

Lynn gasped with excitement. "That's not still standing is it?"

Mel nodded heartily, then said, "No. But there's this new place further up the High Street. We could go there if you like."

"I think I'd like that, Mel," smiled Lynn.

"Excuse me, but are we not forgetting something here?" said Arthur forcibly. "The invasion of English soil by European infidels. The destruction of our sacred Albion Wood. The slaughter of our mythical wildlife."

"Oh yes, Arthur, but it'll wait until tomorrow. Me and Mel have a lot to catch up on," answered Lynn, looking deep into Mel's eyes. He really had been a handsome young man, she mused. A bit of a scrub up and he'd make a presentable old man too.

"But I have formulated a plan to undo this wickedness once and for all," said Arthur heroically.

"Then let us hear it, sire," said Lawrence, bowing his head.

Arthur cleared his throat. "We wait until darkness and attack the building site." There was a tense pause as they waited for him to finish. "OK, I never said it was a well thought-out plan," concluded Arthur.

"Good idea, actually, Arthur. I've spoken to that Mr Morgan and he seems a very diligent and thorough knave," reasoned Lynn. "I'll bet he has evidence about everything he's done somewhere in that office of his. Just in case anyone double-crosses him. Then he won't take the blame alone, you see. I say we build on Arthur's plan and instead of attacking the site, we search it top to bottom for proof."

"Excellent. We leave immediately," ordered Arthur, grasping Excalibur, holding it aloft and knocking a hole in Mel's ceiling. "May God save this night!"

"Tomorrow, Arthur. Lynn and me are off dancing now," said Mel.

"And I have a night of explaining to my parents

about why I'm in no hurry for my PE kit any more," said Gwen.

"I've got maths homework," added Lawrence, pulling a disgruntled face.

"May God save tomorrow night then!" said Arthur proudly, making a second hole in the ceiling.

"After *Coronation Street*," said Mel. The others agreed.

"May God save tomorrow night after *Coronation Street*!" proclaimed Arthur, making a third hole. "We shall meet here at eight. OK Lawrence? Gwen?" Lawrence and his sister nodded. "Mel, Lynn?" The pensioners nodded.

Lawrence's eyes bulged and he leapt up. "It's the prophesy again! Another omen to enforce our claim! Lawrence was nearly wetting himself with excitement by now. "You two didn't fit into the legend alone as we had hoped, but together you do! Together, Mel and Lynn become Mellyn! It sounds almost exactly like Merlin, if you have a speech impediment. Merlin was wizard to King Arthur!'

Gwen didn't turn round, she just banged her head on the window and muckied her forehead.

"Of course!" cried Arthur! "Mellyn! It is *too* much of a coincidence!" (And it was.) Even the pensioners were starting to believe it. "Gwen, you must believe now! Gwen?"

Arthur eyed the room but the depressed teenager had already gone home to face the wrath of her parents. All that remained of her was a message written by finger on the grubby window. Two words. *Jesus wept.*

* * *

The following day, Wednesday, and the sun was as hot as ever. It was ten to nine and the corridors of Bassleton secondary were full of chuckling kids swapping the very latest Arthur King jokes. This was the new buzz. Most people had spent the previous evening phoning, texting and e-mailing each other, recounting the day's events. Arthur King jokes were the new rock and roll.

*Who designed Arthur's round table for him? Sir Cumference.*
*Why isn't Arthur King at school much? Because he doesn't "Come-a-lot".*
*How do Arthur and his knights get ready for bed? With a tin-opener.*

All in all they were some of the lamest gags ever, but today they were spun gold. They had teachers and pupils belly laughing. For this reason, Arthur hid in a toilet cubicle until the nine o'clock bell rang and the corridors were emptying. Thus reducing the cajoling and mickey-taking he'd have to endure.

Arthur was putting his PE/Asda bag into his locker when the jeering of two small first-year girls behind him became too much. He spun round and glared at them, fixing them with the iciest stare he could muster. By George, how those little girls laughed more.

" 'Ere, your Majesty, when one of your knight's dies, what do you put on his gravestone? Is it Rust in Peace?" blurted out the first little girl. Not a clever witticism by any stretch of the imagination, but by now the girls were rolling on the floor.

"And is your house a council castle?" panted the other in between guffaws.

Well, this was more than Arthur could bear. To look incredibly tough he slammed the locker door shut with all his strength, which immediately rebounded from the wooden frame and hit him in the side of the head, knocking him over. This was too much for the cheeky little mockers. The girls crawled away, unable to stand up, their sides fit to split. Arthur lay on the dusty lino floor, nursing the side of his face and staring at the corridor ceiling until the sound of the hysterical little girls had echoed to nothing. A brief flicker of doubt had entered Arthur's mind. Perhaps he *was* being silly? Perhaps his claim to the throne of England was a bit . . . well *daft*?

Then, as though an angel had been sent to assure him in his hour of need, the face of Gwen came into view. She reached down to him.

"Get up, Arthur, you're making the place look untidy."

All doubts were banished from the kingdom of his heart and the warm feeling of sordid schoolboy lust replaced it. Gwen was dressed in jeans and a T-shirt as she wasn't staying in school long today. They walked together to Mr Bedivere's office.

"When I got home the deputy head had been round my house," she said. "He'd calmed down a bit and changed my expulsion to a week's suspension. Purely on the condition that nothing like this ever happens again."

"You mean emergency press conferences?"

"No, I mean me talking to you."

"The impudent dog," snapped Arthur.

"Don't worry, I will. We have a job to do tonight, remember."

They stopped at Mr Bedivere's door, where Lawrence was glumly waiting for Arthur. They had a nine o'clock appointment with the deputy head which would undoubtedly be as pleasant as a visit to the dentist's, Gran's and church all rolled into one. And they were now ten minutes late.

"Right, I'm off to pick up some homework from my form tutor," said Gwen. "It's not a week's holiday, apparently. You two, keep out of mischief and none of your Camelot crud. Keep it zipped about tonight. Got it?"

The two lads nodded and Gwen walked off down the corridor.

"I know what you're looking at Arthur," she said. "Stop it."

He quickly turned and rapped on Mr Bedivere's door.

\* \* \*

Fifteen minutes later the two knights were walking to their respective classes considering how lightly they had got off. A month's detention. It was originally only two weeks, but Arthur had innocently angered the deputy head further by asking for the first week in October and the second week in December. Mr Bedivere immediately doubled the punishment and ordered them to sweep the school corridors every lunch hour for a week as well.

"I'll see you at twelve o'clock then, Lawrence," said Arthur, bracing himself before he entered his maths class. "And remember, keep thine lips sealed about tonight's crusade."

Lawrence dropped to one knee and bowed. Arthur opened the door to the maths class and was instantly greeted by a wall of derisory laughter. He sighed and closed the door behind him. Lawrence expected much of the same in his RE class and glumly walked on. Then, as creepily as the shape-changing T-1000 from *Terminator 2* morphing up from the floor, Fay appeared from behind a wall-mounted firehose and grabbed Lawrence by the collar.

"*What* crusade? What have and your divvy friends got planned?" She fixed him with a blood-curdling stare and Lawrence tried to pull away.

"Get off me, you witch. Get off me or by God's

undies ye shall face my wrath!" said Lawrence meekly.

"Tell me what you're planning to endanger my dad's job again or so help me, Lott, you'll be picking up your teeth with broken fingers."

Lawrence mutely struggled on.

"Fine, have it your way," Fay said, drawing back her fist. But before she could deliver it she felt a tap on her shoulder. She spun round to see Gwen stood holding some books in one hand whilst her other hand raced towards Fay's face.

*Smack!*

Fay flew back, hitting her head against the wall and slid to the floor nursing her bloody snitch.

"Get to class, Lawrence," said Gwen firmly.

Lawrence smiled in absolute awe and admiration of his big sis and her mighty left hook.

"Woah, Gwen, remind me never to read your diary again!"

Gwen winked at him as he scurried to class. She then frowned and whispered, "He reads my diary too?"

"You have made such a mistake, Lott," said Fay. "My mother is on the board of governors of this school."

"Which doesn't really mean anything to me. You see I'm suspended from school so in theory this is outside school hours and therefore nothing to do with your fat cow of a mother." Gwen began walking off. "Oh and if you so much as look at my little brother again, Fay, I will find you and kick bits off you. Got that?" Gwen glared at Fay until she gave an embittered and hateful nod.

Fay watched Gwen walk away and seethed to herself, "Can't promise the same for Arthur King, pet."

With cat-like precision Fay reached for her mobile, flicked open the keyboard and speed-dialled her dad. Upon telling him what she knew, Fay sensed pangs of panic in his voice.

"Sounds like these kids mean business. This is getting too dangerous," he said.

"Dad, they're a couple of stupid kids. This wally Arthur isn't the flipping King of England. The Duke of Dork maybe. Let me have a chat to him, find out what's going on and we can stay one step ahead of them. There can only be a few of those rainbirds left, you can't stop now." There was a pause.

"Fay, I don't know how I came to be what I have become, but I don't like the person I am any more. I need to regain control of my life and that means standing up to you and your mother and the likes of Barry flaming Guthries. Please Fay, it's time for me to make amends. The culling must stop – hello? Fay? Hello?" The click from Mr Morgan's receiver told him Fay had hung up.

He sighed heavily, put down the phone and looked mournfully out of the window. A sickening lump in his throat swelled as he observed Barry Guthries heaving a couple of full bin-liners into a rubbish skip. One of them split when it landed and a puff of blood-stained white feathers billowed out. Mr Morgan wrenched open his office window. "Guthries, get in here, pronto." The thug wafted a feather from in front of his face and mouthed an exasperated expletive.

Once inside the hut, Guthries lounged on the side of Mr Morgan's desk, lighting up a fag while the boss paced the floor nervously. "I've been thinking, Guthries. We should end this here and now."

"Are you breaking up with me, darling?" sneered Guthries. "Men are such pigs." He blew a kiss at his superior.

"I'm serious. I've been pondering what that King Arthur kid said. Eight weeks we've been slaughtering those rainbirds and there's been no rain for eight weeks. It's too much of a coincidence. Supposing they're right?" Morgan shuddered. "It doesn't bear thinking about the damage we've done to the planet already!"

"I get it. You've lost your bottle. I thought this might happen. Your boss, Herr* Mordred, won't be happy. His company's sunk a lot of cash into this project."

Guthries had got up from his seat and was reaching out of the open window for a shovel leant against the hut. Mr Morgan had his back to him, chewing his nails.

"Herr Mordred is a ruthless man and he's

* *Foreign slang for "Mister".*

manipulated me for too long. Sitting in his swanky Brussels office giving his orders down the phone to me. Well not any more. It stops here, Guthries, and I need you as my back-up. Come on, we're going to see Chief Inspector Robertson to get a preservation order slapped on this wood. We can do it if we work together. Are you with me, Barry?"

As he turned to face Guthries Mr Morgan got his answer in the shape of the shovel crashing into his face and rendering him out for the count. Guthries lit his cigarette, sat down and pressed a button on Mr Morgan's phone. After much dialling noise and international beeping the call was answered by a cold and stern foreign accent.

"Greetings, England. How are you, Mr Morgan?" said Herr Mordred.

"It's Barry Guthries again, sir. Mr Morgan's *out* at the moment. I'm afraid the situation we discussed earlier has happened," replied Guthries trying to sound as intelligent as he could.

"My dear boy, how awkward for us both. Will your plan be instigated after all?"

"It will, for the agreed amount. Twenty-five grand paid directly to me once the wood is burned down. English pounds by the way, none of that stupid Euro trash. Then we're done. No more rare birds for you, a little bonus for me." Guthries took a deep breath, nervously awaiting the answer. There was a pause.

"Agreed." Guthries punched the air. "But I want all

the loose ends tied up. And Mr Morgan. What are your plans for him?"

"Let's just say his bonus will be going up in smoke tonight, with the rare birds."

"Impressive. You know, this underhandedness of yours, Barry – it's not very English. We Johnny Foreigners are always led to believe Tommies have a strong sense of fair play and honesty. The bulldog spirit."

Guthries sneered again and said, "What's England ever done for me?"

"It has given you life. Two arms, two legs, a brain, a home and a job," offered Herr Mordred.

A flicker of doubt crossed Guthries's face, and then it was gone.

"Do you want these bleeding birds dead or what?" he snapped.

Herr Mordred laughed, a horrid cold and sinister laugh. "Proceed, Barry, I am pulling your leg. Carry on killing," he said. Then the phone went dead.

A few minutes later Guthries had dumped the still spark-out Mr Morgan in a tool-shed and padlocked it shut. The wound on his head said he was unbelievably dead, but the intermittent movement of his chest suggested otherwise. Guthries kicked dust over the trail of blood leading from the office, then set off to the Griffin for a celebratory pint.

* * *

Lunchtime and the evil school-dinner ladies were serving their unholy meals, chuckling wickedly to themselves. At the end of the hall was the stage and behind the colossal, drawn black curtains Arthur was lazily pushing dust from one spot to another with a broom. Grimy play props, coiled cables and boxes full of costumes were stacked against the walls. Ropes that controlled the curtains and moving scenery hung down from the rafters like spaghetti. Arthur was glad to be concealed from the other pupils as he had heard every possible jibe, gag and one-liner about King Arthur and Camelot so many times. He sighed.

Then suddenly he was no longer alone. Arthur jumped at the sight of Fay, half-sat on a stage-block, looking seductively at him and playfully wrapping her chewing gum around her finger.

"Hi sexy," she purred.

Arthur looked around a few times, then pointed to himself and mouthed the word "*me?*"

"Course you, Arthur." She unbuttoned two buttons on her white blouse and wafted the garment around herself. "Great, isn't it."

"Yeah, it is. It's a fantastic cleavage," said Arthur innocently peering down her blouse. Inwardly Fay was thinking what a complete divvy Arthur was, but outwardly she laughed sexily, determined to get the truth from this utter nincompoop. She pushed him playfully.

"You big flirt. I meant it's great backstage, where

it's cool. Blimey, it's always the quiet ones, isn't it. Mind you, I've been warned about you. Like your women older, don't you. Do you know, we could get up to anything back here and no one would *ever* know?"

"Oh they would, I'd tell them," nodded Arthur. "You don't keep something like that quiet."

She stood up and put her arm round his shoulders and pulled his mouth close to hers. Arthur, despite his loose grip on the way of the world, began to realize that he was being seduced. He broke out into an excited, yet terrified, cold sweat. A flipping fifth-year girl was coming on to him! Him, Arthur King!

"Would you like to meet me tonight? Just me and you?" Her tongue darted out and licked the perimeter of Arthur's lips. He felt quite dizzy. His heart was pounding. For the first time Arthur noticed how devastatingly gorgeous Fay Morgan was. She was a ruddy goddess! Her blood-red lips and pale skin. Her passionate, dark-set eyes and her crafted raven hair. Arthur swayed on the spot, willing himself not to pass out with exhilaration.

"Or," Fay continued in a seductive whisper, "Have you got something else on, because you won't have much on if you meet me, if you know what I mean."

That did it, Arthur grabbed a rope above his head and clung on to it as his legs began to betray him. In a garbled and drooling mish-mash of English, he just about managed to say, "I've got a crusade tonight at Mordred Holdings, but I could meet you after."

It didn't sound much like that, but Fay got the message. Her lips touched his and he felt something shoot into his mouth and caress his tongue. It was her tongue. The blissful wicked kiss lasted a good ten seconds, but to Arthur it was a blink of an eye. He could taste her minty saliva and swallowed it down with an almighty gasp of pleasure.

"What time?" she asked as she stroked his hair and placed gentle bites down his neck.

Here, two things happened simultaneously that negated any chance of the wicked Fay getting her answer. Firstly, Arthur semi-fainted. The displacement of blood coupled with the rush of adrenalin had proven to be too much for his brain and he fell to the floor in a gibbering heap. Secondly, Fay felt her left leg being snatched away from her and the ground rushing up to meet her face at speed. Before she could either scream or hit the deck the ground rushed away again as she was hoisted high into the air and left dangling by a pulley rope. At the same time, the big black stage curtains had parted to reveal the hanging, screaming Fay. Lawrence looked up with smug satisfaction at his handiwork. He had surreptitiously tied one end of the rope to Fay's ankle and the other to a sandbag which, when dropped, pulled the curtains open. The seated pupils in the dining hall erupted with laughter at the sight of the frantic Fay, her skirt round her chest and her *Little Mermaid* knickers showing. Dizzy, furious and in pain, Fay glared down at Lawrence as he bundled

Arthur out of the hall door. She screamed a series of foul and adult swear words at the two of them, but thankfully the expletives (which would have made a checkout girl blush) were drowned out by the bellowing laughter of the pupils.

In the corridor, Arthur snapped. "I was in there, you pillock!"

"No you weren't, Arthur. She was enchanting you! Possessing you!"

"She can flaming well have me!" Arthur stopped dead. "I'm going back." Lawrence grabbed his arm.

"No Arthur, it's the prophesy! Our prophesy. I've been reading up on the legend of King Arthur. There was a sly enchantress called Morgana Le Fay. She's Fay Morgan, daughter of Mr Morgan, our enemy, the advocate of Mordred. It all fits! Get it? God's Gameboy, you're lucky not to be bewitched!" Arthur's eyes bulged. He felt like kicking himself for being so stupid. Mind you, the kiss *was* knockout.

"One good thing came out of it," smiled Arthur. "I've got her chewing gum."

Lawrence winced as Arthur displayed the lump of chewy in his mouth.

# CHAPTER
# TEN

Guthries and his nine key gang members stood around the pool table in the Griffin, each holding a nearly empty pint of lager.* Except for Snooty Bruiser of course, who sipped at his usual medium-sweet sherry. Guthries had drawn a basic map of Albion Wood on the green baize of the table with a blue square of tip-chalk.

"Right, the plan is – these are the three main vehicle routes in and out of Albion Wood. You lot split into three groups and block them off with the wagons, trucks and any heavy machinery you can budge. Make sure nothing with wheels can get into the wood, specifically fire engines," said Guthries with authority.

"You really gonna do it then, Guthries? Burn the flipping place to the ground, to kill them white bird thingies?" asked Pondlife uncertainly.

Guthries nodded and said, "It's the kindest way. Actually it's not, but what do I care. That King

* Well they had had them more than three minutes.

Arthur kid and his friends are still nosing around. The sooner we get the job done the better. And Herr Mordred has offered us all a two hundred quid bonus . . . each." He eyed the gang, carefully hoping that would be enough for them so he could pocket the remainder of the £25,000 bounty. They nodded, impressed.

"So are you all with me?"

Each of the thugs looked to the others, waiting for one to make the first commitment. They all had criminal records. Arson is a serious offence and any one of them getting caught would be looking at five years inside, minimum. No one responded straight away and a moment's silence was broken by Silent Stu carving something on to the fake-oak-panelled pub wall. It read *Letz doit*. Like sheep the others began to agree and offered nods and grunts and sniffs.

"Sounds like rather a jolly wheeze," said Snooty Bruiser.

"Good lads," said Guthries. "We'll wait until it's a bit darker." He patted the enormously fat Child's-Feet next to him. "Child's-Feet, you're round." The gang laughed at the hilarious joke, despite hearing it a thousand times, and Child's-Feet shuffled stupidly off to the bar to get the drinks in. His feet were so small that it took three of his footsteps before his fat body moved at all.

Chief Inspector Robertson walked in through the pub's door and sauntered over to the gang. Planet of the Apes quickly brushed the chalk map off the table before the rozzer reached them. "Well well, lads," smirked Guthries. "We *are* honoured. It's the singing defective. Chief Inspector Robertson, would you like to join us in a drink?"

"I think I'd rather have my eyes sucked out with a vacuum cleaner than drink with dirt like you," said the chief, smiling.

"As you wish, I'm sure Klepto-Col could abstain* you a nice powerful Dyson if you give him five minutes," said Guthries snidely.

The others laughed raucously while the chief took off his copper-topper and put it under his arm.

"I went down to the woods today—"

"Were you sure of a big surprise? 'Cause today's the day the teddy bears have their picnic," interrupted Guthries.

More raucous laughter.

"I was surprised to find work had finished early for the day and Mr Morgan nowhere to be seen," said the chief, ignoring the jibes.

"Went home early, didn't he. He left me in charge so I let the lads knock off early on religious grounds."

"Religious grounds?"

"Yeah, we thought, Jesus, this is hard work, let's go to the pub instead."

Lots more raucous laughter.

---

* *Guthries meant "obtain", but his grasp of basic English was as tenuous as his grasp of right and wrong.*

"The truth, Guthries, please," said the chief firmly.

Still smirking, Guthries replied, "Morgan was ill or something. Bad head."

The chief pulled a puzzled face and asked, "Went home without his car, did he? It's still there."

Guthries's face straightened for a second; he'd forgotten about the boss's car.

"Out of petrol," he said. "Walked home."

"Oh, I see." The chief met Guthries's stare unblinkingly for a moment. "That's fine then. I'll leave you gentlemen to destroy your livers in peace. Evening all."

The chief turned to go. Guthries gave an oink-oink sound. More raucous laughter, but it ended in a flash. Chief Inspector Robertson, despite his fifty-five years, single-handedly took both Guthries's wrists and rammed them up his back, pushing the big youth forward and slamming his face down on the pool table, his nose stuffed down one of the centre pockets.

"Watch your mouth, Guthries, I may be three times your age but my body and brain aren't addled with alcohol. I could take anyone of you losers and not break a sweat. Got that?"

Guthries was in too much pain to answer. The others gulped and stepped back.

"I've got my eye on you," the chief continued, "all of you, and if I think you're up to so much as even scratching your backsides in front of a vicar, I will come down upon you like a tonne of bricks." He let Guthries go. The thug stood up and glared furiously at the policeman. Chief Robertson patted him on the head. "And don't stick your nose down the pockets of a pool table, son, apart from it being very unhygienic, I'm sure it's a foul." With that, the chief replaced his copper-topper atop his head, smiled at the gang and walked out humming the theme tune to *The Bill*.

There was a moment's pause as, again, nobody knew what to say. Child's-Feet shuffled over with a tray full of drinks and asked, "Do you still want pork scratchings, Guthries?"

The big thug furiously swiped the tray up from his hands, showering the room in lager and glass.

\* \* \*

The *Coronation Street* theme began, coupled with the long and lingering hurt look from Deirdre which always signified the end of a scene. Before her mesmerizing chicken neck had faded from the screen, giving way to the credits, Arthur was out the front door and into Mel's. A new cape made from his mother's best rug was safety-pinned to his denim jacket, his double tiara crown hair-gripped into place. Mel and Lynn were ready for action too, armed with torches, a crowbar and a disposable camera. Lynn knew what to expect on these kinds of raids. Arthur nodded proudly at his loyal minions and pulled Excalibur free from it's Asda scabbard, thrusting it triumphantly into the air. On the way to Gwen and Lawrence's house Arthur apologized over and over about the fourth hole he'd put in Mel's living-room ceiling.

"Hmmm," said Gwen's father dubiously as he eyed the odd-looking threesome on his front doorstep. He turned and shouted up the stairs, "Gwen, there's a weird kid and some pensioners to see you."

Gwen swept down the stairs and shut the front door behind her.

"You're grounded, remember," shouted her father as he went back into the living room to shout at *Who Wants to be a Millionaire*. Arthur was about to speak when Gwen gestured for silence. She opened the door again and shouted in.

"Thanks for the book, Arthur. See you next week." She shut the door again and bent over to shout through the letterbox. "Going back to my room, Dad." She put the box lid down gently and ushered the three out of the drive. "He never bothers me when I've got my music on so I've left my CD player on repeat. I've got about forty minutes."

"Hold wench, where be my second, the brave and fearless Sir Lawrence?" demanded Arthur.

"He's crying. Dad really knacked him when Mr Bedivere phoned and told him what Lawrence did to Fay. So he's grounded for as long as me. He's doing some colouring in."

"Let me get this right. We, the Knights of the

Round-ish Table, are about to attack an enemy fortress and save Albion Wood, and my top knight is colouring in?" asked Arthur.

Gwen nodded, Arthur sighed and the four of them carried on walking towards Albion Wood.

From out of the upstairs window of Gwen's house, a pair of watering eyes watched the knights heading for the wood. Lawrence kept looking until they were out of sight. He shuddered one of those shudders you do when you've been crying a lot, then sniffed. He remained looking mournfully out of the window for another twenty minutes until his attention was distracted from self-pity by a large group of ugly young men coming out of the Griffin pub. As they passed by, the orange street-lamp illuminated them and Lawrence recognized them as the labourers from the wood he had seen at the news conference. They were lead by that surly-looking Guthries character and, to his horror, Lawrence realized they too were on their way to Albion Wood. Thinking fast, he ran into his big sister's bedroom and picked up her phone.

\* \* \*

It was very still in the wood and even the mass devastation looked quite picturesque in the dusk. As ever, there were no clouds in the sky and the darkening heavens were becoming peppered with stars and a breathtakingly beautiful harvest moon. Its light gently lit the paths criss-crossing the wrecked woodland. The four reached the main entry gates to the Mordred Holdings work site. Mel's heart was heavy as he gazed at the once-beautiful trees and bushes. Snapped and splintered trees reached up to the sky like thousands of gnarled fingers grasping for a lifeline, a reprieve from this untimely doom. The wood was barely recognizable to the old man. He had spent his youth playing in Albion Wood, but right now it could have been a forest on a dying alien world for all he knew. He was saddened. Plus he needed the loo.

A sturdy-looking padlock hung limply from chains that looped around the large mesh gates. Arthur knew at once what should be done and held Excalibur high.

"No man can keep a king from his destiny, and no man's metal either. Let the breaking of this chain be a symbol of our crusade as Excalibur slices through—"

"Hurry up, divvy," called Gwen. She, Mel and Lynn were walking towards the prefab offices. Lynn had snapped the lock with her crowbar and the gates were wide open. Arthur took a deep breath and slammed the tip of Excalibur into the earth. He missed and left a bruise on his foot five centimetres long. Excalibur, for all its history and magic, was thankfully not that sharp. Arthur gave a tiny "eek" and limped off after his knights.

Lynn turned the handle to Mr Morgan's office. The door opened easily as the unconscious Mr

Morgan – still languishing in the storage shed – hadn't had the opportunity to lock up today.

Soon they were sifting though every file, post-it note and scrap of paper in the bin for some kind of evidence.

"It would help to know what we're looking for," whispered Arthur frantically.

"Records . . . erm . . . transcripts of conversations, photographs even," answered Lynn. "Morgan's corrupt, but he's not stupid. There's always a bigger and more crooked fish round the corner ready to eat you up. He'll have covered his back. I guarantee it."

Mel was examining a computer on Mr Morgan's desk.

"Good thinking, Mel," said Gwen. "It may be on his hard drive. Probably in an encrypted or password-coded file. Is that what you were thinking? Excellent thought."

"I was wondering how you switch this microwave on, actually. There's tea bags and water over there. Thought we'd a have leafy brew," admitted Mel.

"It's a *computer*, Mel," said Gwen patiently as she booted up the system.

Ten minutes later they had found Morgan's personal files. They were pretty much average stuff. Feeble attempts at poetry, vintage computer-game programmes, the odd mucky picture spammed to him by other people. But then they came across a file that they couldn't access.

"This is it, that's what we've been looking for. But

what's the password?" asked Gwen. She typed in a few random words that might be significant to Morgan: **Fay. . . Money. . . Golf. . . Slip-on shoes**.

When she ran out of ideas Mel had a go with words like **Bum, Pants, Wobblies** and other such juvenile expressions someone who's never used a keyboard before might write. He chuckled to himself.

Arthur sat down at the keyboard and took a deep breath. He exercised his fingers like a concert pianist before a big recital.

"I know what it is. In my previous incarnation, my search was for the Holy Grail, the cup that Christ drank from at the Last Supper."

He typed **Grail** in quickly and the screen flashed up: **FILE ACCESSED**. They quietly cheered and patted his back, congratulating Arthur on his ingenuity.

He nodded with satisfaction. "The prophesy holds true once again. Why else would our search for the *grail* have yielded such fruit," said the proud king.

Gwen raised her eyebrows, she knew why. Arthur's typing was atrocious and he'd typed G-A-I-L, which coincidentally happened to be the name of Fay's mum, Gail Morgan. She didn't mention it, deciding Arthur should have at least one great moment.

The information they found was breathtaking. It was everything they wanted to know. Morgan had transcribed the words from every conversation he had had regarding the darker side of the building project. Times and dates of every secret meeting with bent councillors and town planners and the amounts of the bribes they had accepted. Details about the crooked ornithologist who had discovered the white birds to begin with, including how he tried to doublecross Morgan. The bonuses for Mr Morgan, Guthries and several other men to continue the culling in secret. It was dynamite stuff.

Gwen found a floppy disk in Morgan's drawer and downloaded the information. As quickly as they could, they switched off the computer and put everything back just as they had found it.

"Now, all we do is hand this over to the police and this whole disgusting affair will be over," said Lynn. Gwen sighed with relief. It was the end of the nightmare. She could soon return to normality. She smiled for the first time in what seemed like a long time.

Everything was going to be all right.

Wasn't it?

# CHAPTER ELEVEN

**N**ope.

# CHAPTER TWELVE

L ike a wonderful dream blown apart by a parent bellowing in your ear that it's time for school, Gwen's short-lived hope for an end to the adventure was instantly obliterated. As the merry band stepped from the doorway of Mr Morgan's site-hut they were blinded by the site floodlights bursting into life. They shielded their eyes, confused and afraid. From out of the fading glare stepped Barry Guthries and his men, each clutching a sword taken from the skip where the Battle Scar aftershave props had been dumped.

Arthur mouthed something that looked like *Balearics*.

"Well well, lads, a royal visit. It's the king and his Knights of the Round What-not," laughed Guthries nastily as he flicked Arthur's cape with his sword. Mel eased his young friend aside and squared up to Guthries.

"Watch it, lad. I had a bigger breakfast than you. Think you're big, frightening kids and old folk with a ruddy toy sword, do you? Eh? Do you?"

"Of *course* I do. I'm the baddy here, aren't I?" replied Guthries, pulling a puzzled face.

Mel paused. "Up yours," snapped the old guy, stuck for a better answer.

Lynn stepped forward.

"Give it up, son," she said. "We've seen the evidence. It's on the computer."

"I'll just wreck it then," came Guthries, shrugging his shoulders.

"Nah, Guthries," piped up Pondlife, thinking hard. "They can copy it or something. I saw it on a filum.* Aw, what do they call them square things. Erm . . . what's the names."

"Erm . . . not compact discs . . . erm?" offered Child's-Feet.

The Stain suggested, "Wobbly something or another."

Arthur sighed and grabbed the disk off Gwen and held it up.

"They're called floppy disks, you bunch of low-brow morons," he said.

"Thanks," said Guthries, snatching the disk.

Gwen and Lynn growled to themselves. Arthur realized his mistake and kept his gaze from the females.

"Pondlife, you tie them up," ordered Guthries. "Dogga, Planet of the Apes and The Stain, block the main entrance. Mr Bus, Klepto-Col and Silent Stu,

---

* *Thick person's slang for film.*

120

deal with the entrance near the old air-raid shelter. Child's-Feet and Snooty Bruiser, you do the one leading from Ingleby Barwick. Report back here as soon as you're done."

The thugs ran off to be about their misdeeds. Well, Child's-Feet did his best to.

* * *

Ten minutes later, Arthur, Gwen, Mel and Lynn were sat on the riverbank with their hands bound tightly behind their backs and their feet bound at the ankles. A good twenty metres away Pondlife chewed his creepy little fingers nervously as he watched Guthries place two large cans of diesel in Morgan's office, next to a row of ten blasting caps. Guthries put another cap in his pocket and they walked out towards the prisoners.

"I'm not sure about this, Guthries, I've never actually revoked someone's birth certificate* before."

Guthries stopped dead and whispered, "Pondlife, listen to me, there's no going back now. They know exactly what we're up to."

Arthur and co were whispering too, eyeing the bad lads carefully.

"What do you think they're up to?" asked Gwen.

The other three shrugged their shoulders.

Guthries continued, "Those birds are as rare as rocking-horse poo and we've killed hundreds. That's

---

* Thornaby slang for killing someone.

a serious offence and I am not going back inside for anyone. Especially not those four loonies. Two of them are nearly dead anyway. When the bodies are found, or what's left of them, they'll be reported as nuisance tree-huggers trying to save a wood who accidentally got caught in the fire."

Arthur peered intently at Guthries and Pondlife, trying to read their lips, and said, "I think they're saying they're going to let us go or something."

"What about Mr Morgan?" asked Pondlife, nodding to the tool-shed where the unconscious foreman still lay. "He's as crooked as we are. You know the code, Guthries. Wrong 'uns stick together."

Thinking for a second, Guthries decided to lie. "He thinks you're gay," he said.

Pondlife's creepy little jaw dropped.

"I'll kill him myself!" he fumed. Guthries smiled to himself and told Pondlife to keep an eye on the captives while he went to check on the others who were taking too long.

Mel leant over to Gwen, Lynn and Arthur, and whispered, "They're up to no good. I reckon that was petrol they were putting in that office."

Lynn gasped. "Oh God no, they wouldn't! What am I saying, of course they would! They're going to burn down the woods! With us in it! We have to get free!"

"If I could just reach Excalibur, our troubles would be over," said Arthur, looking at his sword lying where Guthries had tossed it, its hilt hidden under the shadow of a thicket of dying bushes. "Mel, Lynn, this is your chance to shine. Use the magical power of Merlin to bring the sword to your king."

Gwen sighed. "Oh ignore him, you two. He's not helping matters by keeping this silly King Arthur business up. What we need to do is—"

Gwen stopped talking when she noticed both Mel and Lynn were staring at the sword, willing it to move.

"Oh for crying out loud," sighed Gwen.

But ever so slightly, the sword *did* move. Then some more.

"Ye gods and little fishes, thy magic works, old wizardy types!" whispered Arthur excitedly.

Gwen was also flabbergasted. The sword rose into the air and stayed there as Fay Morgan, holding the hilt, crept silently through the dead branches.

"We've made a girl appear too! A girl to save us! It's a miracle," gasped Mel.

"That's Fay Morgan, and if she ever did anything for anyone else it'd be more than a pigging miracle," Gwen said, who was disheartened.

Arthur's fear grew rapidly. He was a sitting duck for any reprisal this wicked enchantress wished to evoke.

Fay sneaked over to the four and stood over Arthur drawing back the sword. He gulped and winced as the blade came down between his legs. It severed the ropes that bound his feet.

"Ha! Missed!" sneered Arthur.

"Keep quiet," said Fay. "If you're quick you can get away before they return. No time to explain."

Fay crept away and reached for a heavy-duty sweeping-brush leaning against the skip full of Battle Scar advert props. Circling Pondlife in the semi-darkness Fay drew up close behind him. He was talking to himself.

"I mean, so what if I've never had a girlfriend. That just means I'm ugly. Ugly and nothing else and may the Lord strike me down if it isn't so."

The Lord didn't strike him down, Fay did. The large broom head connected with Pondlife's little head, knocking him out. This was the closest his hair had come to a good brush in years. She ran back to the others whom Arthur had by now freed.

"What are you doing here, Fay?" asked Gwen, suspiciously.

"My dad didn't come home from work and he's not answering his mobile. I'm worried about him. Mum's out late night-shopping in Newcastle so she couldn't help. His car's still here, but I can't find him anywhere. Then I saw you mooching around in the office, then getting tied up by Guthries and his gang. Tut, crusading knights. It's like watching flipping children's television seeing you lot in action." Fay took out her mobile and pressed a number. "I'll try Dad's phone again. Get going." The four didn't move. "Go, go on, get lost before they come back."

"No, fair enchantress, we knights would never desert a damsel in distress. Even a right cow like

124

you. We'll help you find your father, you have my word as a gentleman," said Arthur valiantly, taking a sly look down Fay's top.

Gwen heard a faint ring tone.

"Listen," she said. "It's coming from that shed. Your dad must be in there."

In less than a minute Lynn had prised the lock off the door with Excalibur, (because Arthur wasn't strong enough) and the unconscious Mr Morgan was woken. He was dizzy and disorientated, but better than he looked. While a tearful Fay dressed a deep gash on her father's forehead with the arm off her blouse he explained all that had gone on about the culling of the birds, the back-handers and bribes and Herr Mordred orchestrating it all from his plush Brussels office.

"Herr Mordred, eh?" said Arthur, nodding. "This fiend doth well to stay in Europe far away from the justice of my metal!" Arthur raised his hand into the air and wondered why his sword wasn't in it. Lynn tapped his shoulder and handed him Excalibur. Arthur was going to do it again but the moment was gone.

"Well I'm in no position to judge, Arthur. I owe you kids a great apology, but a bigger thanks for making me see reason," added Mr Morgan. "And before those yobs can do any more damage, I'm phoning Chief Inspector Robertson and spilling the beans." He held up his mobile phone and flipped open the keyboard.

A swishing sound came from nowhere and suddenly the phone was wrenched out of Mr Morgan's hand. It shot to the ground, impaled with a crossbow bolt through its centre.

Collectively the good guys swung round to see Guthries on one knee, still aiming the deadly device at them.

"You lunatic, Guthries. You could have killed me!" Mr Morgan shouted.

"What are you talking about," the thug replied as they all descended the riverbank and stepped through the water, "I was *trying* to kill you. I'm just a lousy shot, remember."

"We cannot be taken hostage again, men. Oh, and lasses. Grab a weapon and defend thine selves!" barked Arthur, pointing to the skip full of swords and shields. They didn't need telling twice. Mel, Lynn, Mr Morgan, Fay and Gwen armed themselves and stood awaiting the approach of the laughing thugs.

"Look at that, they want a sword fight," belly-laughed The Stain.

"Then it'd be tremendously rude of us to disappoint them. Come on, chaps, let's cut them to ribbons," said Snooty Bruiser with a look of sadistic excitement on his face. The rest of the mob ran up the other side of the bank to do battle with the good guys.

Arthur pointed directly at Guthries and said, "Save the ugliest one for me!' He jumped down the riverbank and splashed into the water. Guthries chuckled at the insult. He tossed his crossbow aside and took out the sword held in his jeans' belt-loop.

"Let's do it, kidda," laughed Guthries. "Sorry – your Majesty." Guthries grunted as he brought his sword down towards Arthur's head, but the thirteen year old raised Excalibur and parried the first attack, stopping it dead. Guthries was genuinely impressed. He held his sword with two hands and sideswiped at Arthur who again blocked the attack. All that practice with T-squares was paying off, but this was still just a silly kids' game to Guthries. He laughed heartily at the guts of the youngster-who-would-be-king. Using his greater weight, Guthries lashed out with three massive blows. Arthur stopped each of them, but was driven to his knees. Before a fourth arrived, Arthur thrust Excalibur forward in an upwards arc, plunging the blade into Guthries's thigh. The big thug roared and fell into a sitting position in the beck, grasping his leg. Blood oozed from the wound and suddenly this was no longer child's play.

This was real.

Cursing like a barmaid, Guthries stood back up and lunged his sword at Arthur, the blade heading for his stomach. The determined hero deflected the blow by sideswiping it away with Excalibur and both swords slid against each other, sparking until the hilts met and the two warriors were face to face. Arthur could smell the booze on Guthries's breath.

The bigger man, far stronger, clamped his hand round Arthur's neck and bent him backwards, buckling his spine. In an un-gentlemanly move (but then his opponent was far from a gent), Arthur raised his left knee and clobbered Guthries in the crotch. He bellowed like a wounded beast.

Elsewhere in the escalating battle Mr Morgan had a sword in each hand and was duelling as best he could. He was still groggy from the shovel blow. He took on Snooty Bruiser and Dogga with his left hand and Klepto-Col and Silent Stu with the other. They were half his age, but not a quarter as fit. The lure of booze had taken its toll on the nineteen year olds just as it had on their leader. They fought breathlessly and awkwardly.

Gwen was engaged with The Stain. She had managed to land several firm prods with her sword, but they failed to penetrate the caked-on filth in the fabric of his clothes. They made his sweatshirt and jeans as tough as chain-mail armour. Fay was no fighter and cursed her limp girly wrists as she tried to swing a mace at her opponent. She wasn't built for this, she told herself. She was designed to *attract* boys, not fight them off! Luckily Child's-Feet, with whom she was skirmishing, couldn't move as dextrously as she, so the battle was quite evenly matched. Mel and Lynn fought as one. She held a shield across them both while he poked the sword round the side of it at Planet of the Apes. They had picked the worst form of defence for such a chimp-like enemy. His long arms could easily reach to jab a long dagger back over their shield and both of them were sustaining many a nasty little nick.

Mr Bus wasn't yet in the barney. He was late, as usual, because he hadn't liked the choice of sword someone had handed him earlier and was rifling round the skip for a "nicer one". He kept shouting over that he wouldn't be long and they should carry on without him for now.

Arthur had really hurt Guthries and the big thug was on his knees in the water, doubled over, eyes slammed shut in severe discomfort. Arthur had flicked Guthries's sword away out of reach with his own and turned to run up the bank to help his fellow knights out. No sooner had he reached the top when felt a massive weight on his back and a big arm round his neck.

"Oh no you don't, you little swine!" snarled the thug. But Guthries lost his footing in loose mud and he fell back down the bank, dragging Arthur with him like a rag doll and flipping him head-first towards the water. Arthur felt like he was in slow motion because before he landed in the beck he saw Excalibur fly out of his hand and crash against a large rock on the riverbed. The tip of the sacred sword shattered off.

"Nooooooooooooooooo!" yelled the king, then, "Blub-a-blub-a-blub!" as he slammed face-down in the water. Then Guthries landed on him, knocking the air out of his lungs. The brute had found himself in an ideal position to finish off the boy-king once and for all, and he pushed his face hard into the muddy riverbed. Arthur used what little might he had left to pull his head up and grab small gasps of air before Guthries kept ramming it back down. In between duckings Arthur caught glimpses of the fight atop the riverbank and his heart sank to see that his knights were now losing the battle. Again the whole scene seemed set in slow motion. Arthur saw Mr Morgan lose his balance and fall under four of the thugs as they dropped their swords and rained punches down upon him.

Back down! Splash!

When he managed to look back up he saw Gwen lose her weapon and try to deflect a slash of The Stain's sword with her hand, gashing it.

Back down! Splash!

Arthur saw Fay take a rap to the face from Child's-Feet's elbow and crumple to the floor, crying.

Back down! Splash!

Arthur saw Mel land a daring head-butt on Planet of the Apes, but then reach for Lynn. She was on the floor grasping her chest with an attack of angina.

Back down! Splash!

Had the breaking of Excalibur ended the prophesy? Broken the enchantment somehow? Arthur prayed for salvation. He roared to the moon to send his warriors some succour.

And it came.

# CHAPTER THIRTEEN

From out of the trees came the call. The sound of a battle-horn rang out. Stood at the mouth of Albion Wood was the finest sight Arthur had ever witnessed. It was Lawrence and an army of around twenty first-year boys silhouetted against the moon! He was stood before them, resplendent in his new home-made battle armour. A tough cape made from his mum's best lounge rug and a helmet that had once been an orange bucket. He'd cut a square section from it so he could see out. In one hand he held an aluminium ornamental curtain rail as his trusty new lance. In the other, the battle horn (a traffic cone he'd found on the way). Sir Lawrence-a-Lott had raised a legion of first-year boys by ringing round and offering each of them a free five-minute rummage in his sister's underwear draw on condition they meet at Albion Wood to fight some teenagers. Each one agreed instantly.

And here they were, Lawrence's new model army. A row of enthusiastic young lads ready to fight like warriors for nothing more than a root round a knicker drawer. Noble men indeed. Each one with the cross of St George applied to their faces in Gwen's expensive red lipstick. Behind Lawrence stood Ste Jukes and on his shoulder sat Deformed Terry, a look of tough determination on both of his faces.

"Charge!" bellowed Lawrence and every man-jack of them ran into the wood to join the battle.

On the ground Pondlife opened his boggle eyes and blinked. "What happened?" he croaked. Dazed, and with a searing pain in his head, he sat up and was instantly trampled back to unconsciousness by the rampaging first years. The cheering eleven year olds grabbed a sword each from the skip (where Mr Bus was still searching for one for himself) and ran to the battle. The excited kids began fighting with the fiery vigour of men on a promise of seeing a bra. Deformed Terry sprang into action too. He leapt on to Dogga's face and dug both sets of teeth into his cheeks. This was poetic justice from the animal kingdom. Payback for all the dogs Dogga had bitten over the years. Dogga clawed at the rat, trying to pull the thing from himself, and fell backwards down the riverbank.

Gwen's hand was bleeding and she felt sick and cold. She gripped it hard, blocking out the pain, and charged back into the battle. With her other hand she picked up stones and threw them at the bad guys, successfully hindering them in their individual tussles.

Mr Morgan thought he was hallucinating when he

saw his three remaining attackers – Snooty Bruiser, Klepto-Col and Silent Stu – being pulled away from him like peel from a satsuma by a crowd of young boys. Each one of the thugs was hurled to the ground and severely dealt with by two or more lads.

Fay was up and battling again after Child's-Feet's blow to her face. The fury caused by her make-up being ruined was enough to get her back in the game and she kicked Child's-Feet's diminutive hooves from under him.

"Lynn!" wailed Mel as he held her in his arms, panic filling his heart.

"Got a bit of a dicky ticker, Mel. Didn't want to bother you with it," she said through pain-gritted teeth.

"I'll get you out of here. I'm not losing you again! I'll carry you!"

Lynn half smiled at the determined old gent as he tried to lift her up, then scowled as he dropped her when his back went.

Arthur was still on his front, but no longer drowning. Guthries was now stood up, his attention taken by the sight of the young knights destroying his men. And if Arthur hadn't said, "Hello, I *am* still here" in a cocky tone, Guthries may well have forgotten all about him. The big bad lad snarled and turned to the young king.

"Oh knackers," said Arthur thinking he maybe should have kept shtum. Guthries grabbed the back of Arthur's head and forced his face underwater again. The young lad gritted his teeth and tried to fight back, but Guthries's strength was now stronger, fuelled by pure anger.

And then he let go.

Just like that.

Arthur looked up to see Chief Inspector Robertson had leapt down the riverbank feet-first and knocked Guthries over into a bundle on the riverbank. The chief turned to Arthur and with one hand pulled him up.

Confused but grateful, Arthur observed five other police officers grappling with Guthries's gang. It was harder for the lawmen and -women to stop the first years trying to run the thugs through than to handcuff the actual bad guys. Arthur spat silt and mud from his mouth and the chief patted his back.

"Easy lad, get your breath. Guthries'll do you no more mischief," said the chief.

He then noticed the puzzled look on Arthur's face and followed his gaze to the riverbank where Guthries had been a few seconds earlier. He was gone.

Looking up to the hut complex, Arthur screamed for everyone to take cover because Guthries was priming a blasting-cap. "He's got petrol in there! Get down!"

"You've won the battle, King Arthur, but not the war! Say goodbye to your precious rainbirds!" snarled Guthries. He threw the blasting cap into the office, smashing the window, and dived into the trees. Everyone dropped to the ground and covered their heads and ears.

Then all hell broke loose.

For a split-second the office hut seemed to swell like an inflated balloon. Then its seams split and a bright orange light shone though. A millisecond later the entire structure was engulfed in a fireball, almost atomizing it. A terrifying shower of ignited diesel shot upwards in every direction and only then did the sound come. A simultaneous crack, boom and fizz. Everywhere was showered with small drops of burning diesel like a vengeful downpour of Satanic rain. Dry tree trunks, mounds of crisp dead bushes, desiccated roots and stems instantly combusted. Small fires ignited everywhere. The clothes of a couple of people were flecked with tiny droplets of liquid fire. They instinctively rolled in the dust, easily putting them out. Fay noticed Mel's back was alight as he had used himself as a shield for his beloved Lynn. She pushed the old man over, deadening the fire.

Chief Inspector Robertson was on his feet first and bellowing into his police radio for assistance from the fire brigade, taking absolute charge of the situation.

"Listen to me, all of you! Grab shovels, swords, anything, and beat out as many fires as you can!" He turned to the remainder of Guthries's gang, who were huddled together, shaking and sobbing like frightened children. "You lot, earn yourselves a lighter sentence and get this fire out!" They nervously nodded in agreement and joined in the fire fighting.

Lawrence ran to Arthur and helped him to his feet and gasped, "Sire, do you live?"

"Aye, Sir Lawrence-a-Lott. I'm not ready for old Avalon yet." He hugged his young friend. "I like your helmet, by the way."

Lawrence proudly patted it and said, "Cheers. Mam's going to knack me though. And Gwen for that matter."

"Gwen! Where is she?" said Arthur seriously, belatedly remembering his queen. To their horror they saw Guthries, now across the beck and high up the far end of Albion Wood, running for his life. And with him, being dragged behind by her arm, was Gwen!

"He's got my sister!" screamed Lawrence. He started to give chase but Arthur stopped him.

"No, Lawrence. He's mine." Arthur turned on his heels, bounded up the bank and pursued them at speed, his broken sword Excalibur in hand.

Guthries ran blindly into the darkened wood, unsure of his route, pulling Gwen in each direction. She was crying and screaming protests, but the thug was oblivious to her distress. He stopped to catch his breath and to get his bearings. Disorientated by adrenalin and rage, he tried to concentrate. Which was the way back to the pub and his car?

"Think!" he roared to himself. There! By the old air-raid shelter, that was it. If he bore right from there and followed the beaten path he would come out within a stone's throw of the pub.

"Get off me, you big idiot! It's over, right! You lost!" yelled Gwen.

"You ruined everything!" he growled. "You're staying with me until I'm a hundred miles away from this mess!" He strode on, pulling Gwen behind him. The girl caught her foot on a tree root and fell forward, knocking them both to the floor. Guthries swore and got up. He reached down for Gwen again but before he could, Arthur's foot connected with his hand, knocking it away, and the jagged end of Excalibur dug into Guthries's bloated belly.

"Touch her again and I'll lop your fat pig's head clean off," shouted Arthur.

"Oh you're a welcome sight, Arthur," seethed Guthries sarcastically. He sideswiped the sword away and swung a punch which connected with Arthur's mouth, splitting his lip and knocking him off his feet.

"If I ever see you again, son, I swear I will kill you!" He kicked Arthur hard in his side, then ran from the wood.

Gwen crawled over to Arthur, who was lying on his side, crying. She smiled down at him and brushed bloody leaves and dirt from his face.

"Arthur! You came to rescue me! Thank you. You're such a brave kid." She hugged him. Lawrence ran up and knelt beside them. He was elated that his sister and his king were both OK.

"The coppers and our fellow knights have got the blaze pretty much under control and the fire brigade will finish it off. Where's Guthries?'

"Legged it! It's over, Lawrence! We won. We saved the wood! Thanks to you two!" said Gwen emotionally.

"Nah. Thanks to King Arthur here. You did it, sire. You saved old Albion." Lawrence took off his bucket helmet. "We can rest now, Arthur, our work is done."

"No."

Gwen and Lawrence look puzzled as Arthur got to his feet shakily.

"He insulted you, Gwen. Manhandled you, and that is bad enough. But worse, he betrayed Albion. He tried to sell out a piece of England. People like Guthries just take from their countries. Take and complain and never give back. Well he'll pay now, in full. I won't rest until he has. It's now a crusade." Arthur picked up Excalibur and dipped his finger into the blood coming from his bust lip. He drew a blood-red line down the centre of his face and another across it. The cross of St George in blood. He began walking after Guthries. Gwen yelled after him.

"Arthur, no! The police will pick him up!"

The king turned and smiled heroically at her.

"No, my queen. The police will pick up what is left of the knave." And off he strode towards his destiny.

* * *

In the unlit car park of the Griffin public house a lumbering, exhausted figure ran into the car park towards a vulgarized, body-kit car. Guthries slammed the key into the door and got in as fast as he could. He fumbled for the ignition key and, unable to find it straight away, beat the steering wheel hard over and over. He stopped, tried to calm himself, and checked his mirrors to make sure he was alone. In front of his car was the high, red-brick car park wall. Behind him and to the left were other parked cars. To the right, the pub. There were no security lights in the car park, making parts of it pitch black. A cloud of steam wafted from the pub's kitchen fans and over the bonnet of Guthries's car, making the whole scene very *downtown-Gotham-City-esque*.* He wound down the window and listened hard. The faint chatter from the pub and occasional clanking of plates from the kitchen was all he could hear. He took a deep breath, found the key and put it in the ignition.

Before he could turn it he was terrified by a massive "bang" from his bonnet. Through bulging eyes he saw the figure of Arthur King stood on the front of his car after having leapt down from the wall. His blanket cape settled behind him, fanning the steam aside, and in a moment he drew back Excalibur. Guthries just had time to shield his eyes

* *To coin a phrase no one will ever use again.*

as the sword shattered his windscreen, showering him in tiny cubes of glass.

Guthries looked up, but Arthur was gone. Leaping out of the car he looked around, but there was no sign of the thirteen year old. By now his racing heart echoed inside him like some frantic machine. Then came Arthur's voice, as silent as a whisper, but oh so sinister.

"Oi, traitor."

Guthries turned quickly for the source of it and saw Arthur's dark figure duck behind a Ford Mondeo. Guthries dropped to the floor and looked under the car, seeing nothing. There came a swooshing sound and Guthries felt something jab in his back. Arthur had run over him, using him as a springboard to leap back into the shadows. By the time Guthries stood up, the youth was gone again. Guthries was now more scared than furious.

"Coward," came Arthur's voice. Guthries swung round and saw Arthur disappear into the steam. Thinking he'd got him cornered in the doorway of the pub's back doors, Guthries ran at a dark shape just beyond the steam and grabbed it. He stumbled to the ground as the shape fell apart in his arms. A pile of empty beer crates. He tried to pick himself up. The swooshing of Arthur's cape came once more as he darted through the blackness. Guthries decided he had had enough. He ran to his car, wrenched open the boot and pulled out a handgun he'd bought from Pondlife earlier that day. He'd never fired a gun before, but he was more than prepared to have a bash now.

"I warned you, Arthur," yelled Guthries into the night, looking all around himself. "I said I'd kill you, and I will."

No response.

"Where are you, Arthur?"

No response.

Then. . .

"Here, scoundrel."

Guthries spun round and discharged the gun. There was a loud bang, a flash and something fell over in the dark.

"Got you, you little git!" laughed Guthries nervously. From out of the darkness, from the spot where the thing fell over, he heard Arthur groan with pain. Running to the sound, Guthries reached down for the shape on the floor, only to find an empty wheelie bin with a large smoking hole in it. "Huh?" gasped Guthries.

"Just kidding," said Arthur, stepping out from behind Guthries.

The thug spun round to face his enemy and the last thing he saw, besides Arthur's smile, was the hilt of Excalibur glint in the moonlight a second before it connected with his temple, knocking him over . . . and out.

Arthur flipped the sword up in the air and caught it the right way round. "Well Arthur," he said to himself, "You may or not be a king, but you're surely a man. Only thirteen and already you've had your first fight in a pub car park. *Smart*."

# EPILOGUE

A few days later, tales of the amazing battle to save Albion Wood were fading into folklore. The best news was that the wood was saved and building work stopped permanently. Mr Morgan, still in police custody, had told all about the conspiracy and a preservation order was placed on Albion Wood. Mr Evans, the crooked ornithologist, had been arrested and all of Guthries's gang were facing prison sentences, but not as hefty as the foul ringleader's would be. Worse for Guthries was that it had come to light Herr Mordred was paying him twenty-five grand when he'd only offered his gang a measly pittance by comparison. Even when he got out of jail he wouldn't dare show his face in Thornaby again. He'd broken the criminal code and swindled his own. He was now an outcast. A marked man.

"I've put in a word for Morgan," said the chief, as he, Gwen, Mel and Lynn strolled in the warm Saturday morning sunshine through Albion Wood. "I think he'll get a reduced sentence, but he's a better man for it, that I do know."

The wood was already looking healthier. The charred remains of the hut complex had been cleared away. In fact nearly all sign of Mordred Holdings had vanished. There were patches of new greenery bursting through everywhere. The four walked slowly on, Mel watching Lynn's every move with trepidation.

"You OK, love? You don't need a rest?" he asked.

"Yes, Mel, a rest from your flaming fussing," sighed Lynn. "Honestly, Chief, he's watching over me like a weirdo watches trains."

"You've spent the last two days in hospital, woman!"

"Mel, it was a slight scare. I'm fine. Got to keep sword-fighting down to a minimum from now on though."

They laughed.

Gwen was holding a dog lead with twin collars on the end around Sir Deformed Terry.* The brave little rat was fully recovered from his battle and both his faces seemed contented as the last of the diggers trundled past on the back of a yellow truck.

"Good riddance an' all," said Mel, sticking two fingers up at the driver.

"Ditto," said the chief, doing the same. The driver looked hurt and drove on.

"You know, we should really finish on a song," said the chief.

---

* After the battle, Arthur had knighted everyone who'd fought for Albion Wood and that included Deformed Terry. The odd little rat had even been given a mooch round Gwen's underwear drawer like the other knights.

Mel, Lynn and Gwen stopped dead in their tracks behind him. *Oh no, not a song!* they collectively thought. The chief carried on walking. "In honour of our young hero, Arthur. I've worked out new lyrics to 'Killer Queen', which I've cleverly re-titled 'Killer King'. I'll sing it first and you pick it up as you go. A one, a two, a one-two-three. . .

*"He's a killer king,*
*Not that he'd kill anything,*
*Dynamite with an old found sword,*
*Guaranteed to save your woods,*
*Anytime!"*

Mel and Lynn rolled their eyes at one another and followed, trying to repeat the words. Gwen smiled and stayed where she was. She gazed around the regenerating Albion Wood, still unable to take in everything that had happened to her recently. She had had a full apology from Mr Bedivere and her week's suspension quashed. Everything was back to normal. Mel even said that the cat's head was no longer grinning, if you can call that normal. She shuddered at the thought of it.

Then something moved in the tree above her. She glanced up, half expecting to see to see a rainbird roosting in the green leaves, safe and content at last. But that's not what she saw. She yelped and her heart jumped.

"Morning, fair lady," came the voice of Arthur.

Both he and Lawrence were crouching on a thick branch, gazing down at her. Gwen instinctively stepped back and, knowing Arthur, checked all the buttons were fastened on her top. Both lads were dressed entirely in green. Aerosol-sprayed green trainers, green wool tights, green rugby shirts and green baseball caps with green feathers sticking out of each. They held staffs whittled from long branches. There was a pause as Gwen tried to comprehend what she was seeing.

"We're wearing lasses' tights and Arthur said it feels sexy," said Lawrence. Arthur shot him an angry glare.

"Why?" asked Gwen blankly.

"Robin Hood at your service, my lady," Arthur said proudly. "Well, I do live in Sherwood Road, don't I? Sherwood Road, Sherwood Forest. You can't argue with coincidence, can you."

"It makes perfect sense, sis," added Lawrence, "We've fulfilled our Arthurian calling, so this is our next mission. Although I haven't quite worked out who I am yet. But I'm in there somewhere, isn't that right, Arthur?"

"No doubt about it, Lawrence. We are the re-incarnations of those merry men who bounded from tree to tree righting wrongs."

"Ste Jukes isn't, though," said Lawrence determinedly. "He shaved his head so he could be Friar Tuck and we told him to grow up. Didn't we, Arth?"

"Yeah. You can't crowbar people in, that'd be just silly."

Gwen wondered if she should explain what irony was. But didn't bother.

Both lads leapt out of the tree simultaneously. Instead of landing like heroic woodsmen of yore, on their feet and ready for action, they flopped stupidly into heaps making wimpish "oof" and "gaah" noises. Arthur even rolled on to a nettle and screamed like a lady.

They eventually got up.

"You fit in though, Gwen. You're my Maid Marian, because," he sang, "*Everything I do, I do it for you*." He paused for her reaction, but none came. "Will you be her, Gwen, a damsel worth fighting for?"

"No, Arthur."

"Oh." He looked to the ground. There was a pause. "I know you think I'm a bit of a divvy, and that I'm too young for you, but this won't always be the case. One day I'll be worthy of you, Gwen, I swear it." He thought for a second, then half-heartedly added, "And the same age as well."

Gwen smiled sweetly at him. "You're a very special person, Arthur King," she said. "And I am very proud to know you." She kissed him on his cheek and walked on to join the others. "And stop looking at my bum," she added.

Arthur quickly looked at Lawrence who was wiggling his eyebrows.

"Woah, she *kissed* you. You are *seriously* in there, Arth— Sorry – Rob."

"She loves me, she just doesn't realize it yet. OK, let's go and rob from the rich and give to the poor. What do you suggest?"

Lawrence thought for a second. "Let's nick some milk from a doorstep and give it to the first baby we see."

"A noble quest!" said Arthur.

The two heroes of the forest ran into the trees, merging with the reviving green of the leaves in search of action, adventure and someone's semi-skimmed.

Above them, in the sky, things were moving. Clouds were forming. Dark clouds. Beautiful dark rain clouds. And gliding round and round them were young fledgling rainbirds flying freely in safety for the first time in such a long time.

Then something very wonderful happened.

It started to rain.

Was this proof positive rainbirds do control the rain? Or was it just another damn coincidence?

Ye End
of

*The Legend of Arthur King.*

# ABOUT THE AUTHOR

Dean Wilkinson began writing comedy in children's comics which saw him publish his own title *Fizog* – it lasted a staggering three issues. He turned his attention to telly and went on to pen episodes and sketches for many shows including *Smith & Jones*, *The Brian Conley Show*, *The Big Breakfast*, *Zig & Zag*, *Byker Grove*, *Timmy Towers*, *Comic Relief*, *Laugh Out Loud* etc. He wrote for many years for Ant and Dec, scripting series such as *The Ant And Dec Show*, *Unzipped*, *Friends Like These* and most successfully the multi-award-winning *SMTV Live*, for which he wrote *Chums*, *Cat and Dog*, *Dec Says*, *Poke-rap*, *SMTV 2099* to name just a few little gems. He is also the creator and writer of BBC TV's *Bad Penny*. Dean lives on Teesside in the north of England with his wife and daughters.

Keep an eye out for the return of Arthur and co in the sequel to this book. . .

# ARTHUR KING
## AND THE
## CURIOUS CASE OF THE TIME TRAIN

There's odd things happening in Thornaby, again. For a start, time doesn't seem to be going as it ought to. Rips in the very fabric of time are leaving bewildered people hours out of sync with their lives. One naughty boy found himself in trouble he shouldn't have been in for a whole day and Lawrence got mugged by cavemen.

Then there's the strange nightly rumblings underneath the town. Some say the Ghost Train is back, a distantly remembered legend about a train that arrives in the night to take dead souls to their final resting place.

More importantly, for Arthur at least, is the fact he still hasn't got off with Gwen. Plus she has a stupid girly crush on her handsome Physics teacher, Mr Toppol. Arthur and Lawrence embark on an adventure more perplexing and frightening than the great Sherlock Holmes and Watson ever did, where they. . .

- uncover a link between the Ghost Train and the Time Rips;
- come up against the insane Cult of Temporal Renewal, who want an end to modern life;
- and face a foe whose birth certificate should have expired nearly a hundred years ago!